Loopholes

Loopholes

Showey Yazdanian

QUATTRO BOOKS

The publication of *Loopholes* has been generously supported by
the Canada Council for the Arts and the Ontario Arts Council.

  Canada Council   Conseil des Arts
for the Arts   du Canada

 ONTARIO ARTS COUNCIL
CONSEIL DES ARTS DE L'ONTARIO
an Ontario government agency
un organisme du gouvernement de l'Ontario

Author photo: Laura Yazdanian
Editor: Luciano Iacobelli
Cover design and typography: Natasha Shaikh

Library and Archives Canada Cataloguing in Publication

Yazdanian, Showey, author
        Loopholes / Showey Yazdanian.

ISBN 978-1-927443-78-1 (pbk.)

        I. Title.

PS8647.A94L66 2015   C813'.6   C2015-902327-0

Published by Quattro Books Inc.
Toronto
www.quattrobooks.ca

Printed in Canada

loop•hole / 'lūp-ˌhŌl / *n.* 1 GAP IN LAW a small mistake or omission in a rule or law that allows it to be circumvented 2 A PASSAGE FOR ESCAPE A passage for escape ; means of escape 3 SLIT IN WALL a small aperture in a wall, through which small arms are fired at an enemy.

Terms and Conditions

The loopholes contained within are entirely fictional. Your use of any information or material is entirely at your own risk, for which the author shall not be liable. Once you have read *Loopholes* (hereinafter "the novel"), it constitutes a legally binding agreement. By reading it, you implicitly promise to treat all characters and plots as fictional and understand the potential consequences of not doing so. If you have reason to treat the novel as fact rather than fiction, the author will not be responsible for any losses either actual or anticipated. Information within the novel may contain technical inaccuracies or typographical errors. Information may be changed or updated without notice. The author may also make improvements and/or changes to the novel at any time without notice. Unauthorized use, hacking, vandalism or financial fraud arising from reading this novel may result in a claim for damages and/or be a criminal offence. This story contains material which is owned by or licensed to the author. This material includes all characters, words and punctuation used in the novel. Reproduction is prohibited other than in accordance with the copyright notice, which forms part of these terms and conditions. All trademarks reproduced in this novel which are not the property of, or licensed to, the author are acknowledged as such. From time to time this novel may also include references to other novels. These references are provided for your convenience to provide further information. They

No lawyers were harmed in the writing of this work of fiction.

Part 1:

Lives of Quiet Desperation
Toronto

Chapter 1
The Pyramid Scheme

By my sixth week of law school, I knew precisely how everyone in it would spend the rest of their lives. The foundations of a caste pyramid, faintly perceptible even on the first day of classes, cemented rapidly into a veritable Cheops of social status. The dim and spotty masses with gingivitis, the ones who'd squeaked in off the waiting list, languished at the base. The pointy tip contained the handsome ones, the slim ones, the smooth-skinned smooth-talking strawberry smoothies.

The *crème de la crème* of this lot – the one percent of the one percent – shot across the border to the big New York law firms within five minutes of graduation, renouncing their citizenships during layovers in Chicago. Toronto burns with envy for New York; New York is Toronto with fox-furs and a tiara. Absolutely, say the snotty memsahibs of Yorkville, I was in New York for the weekend, I went to Magnolia Bakery and snorted a cupcake. How sinful! We Canadians love boasting about our health care and our social safety net and *notre très Européen* Montréal, but show a hotshot Toronto lawyer a flash job in Manhattan and he'll board the next American Airlines flight whistling "Yankee Doodle Dandy." It's not personal: it's just freezing up here.

The rest of the pyramid's tip-dwellers walked in beauty on Bay Street (Wall Street's eager, bumptious little sister) and sipped money from crystal goblets. I wish I could tell you what else they did on Bay Street, but if it isn't obvious yet, I frankly have no idea. I'm five foot four, sour-faced and sweaty; every dress shirt I have ever owned is dotted with Jackson Pollock driblets of perspiration. Next to the seven-foot Confidence Men who lope around boardrooms in scented mists of aftershave, I look like Dobby the House Elf.

Take Blake, for instance. Blake was broad and tanned with nice green eyes. He played hockey for the varsity team and to sustain the handsome bulk that filled his sporty zip-up hoodies, he ate constantly: nuts and dates and some stuff in sacking that was possibly hay. He knew I hated him, but he still bumped fists whenever we met. Blake now works for Sullivan Phelps, the slickest firm in the city, and when he isn't busy diddling people he drives his Lexus in circles around the other fat mansions above St. Clair Avenue.

Confidence Men are not infrequently female, and Michelle is a prime example. "Shell," as we were exhorted to call her, was five foot seven and a delicate shade of blonde. To offset her *Faerie Queene* looks she wore big square black glasses and got an A-double-plus in absolutely everything. She chaired the Executive Student Committee and played golf in tight but tasteful jerseys and addressed everyone in a smooth polite voice. I loved her. I hated her too. She works for Smith Johnson, another oil-slick outfit, and now lives smoothly ever after in a two-level condo on the lake with her investment banker husband.

Confidence Men can even be black. Bay Street and Wall Street and their eventual terminus, Easy Street, aren't deliberately racist. There's no need for it: smooth cocksure faces, whether black or white or brown or golden, somehow all acquire the same rich, fleshy hue when stuffed into a thousand-dollar suit. It isn't race they object to, it's *irregularity*. Black may be beautiful, but Ghanaian kufi hats are not. The Arab oil boys are good business; Sudanese dishdashas are best stashed in the back. And so on, and so forth. The object of the game is *sameness*. The same golf handicaps. The same cars. Even the same affairs – but never mind that for now.

Mohamed is an excellent specimen of what passes for unorthodoxy in the *monde de la crème*. Black-bearded Mohamed chaired the Smithy Mock Trial competition, played kooky ukulele at the yearly talent show and graduated with the Gold Medal. My hatred of Mohamed was boundless. That bastard clerked for the Supreme Court. I have no idea of what he does now, or of the square footage of his lovely house, or of the precise shade of his girlfriend's pert areolae, but I'm quite confident that I would detest him for all of it.

The remaining ninety-five percent of the class was a motley assortment of dullards and grubs: the unremarkable and the unspeakable. The ones who pursed their lips whenever someone told a really good racist joke and then repeated the joke, outraged, to anyone who would listen usually ended up working for the government. Government lawyers enjoy middling prestige, comfortable but not lavish salaries and near infinite holidays. The mere act of working for government is practically a holiday in itself: there's never any particular rush to do anything, and no one cares in the slightest if your client, the Canadian taxpayer, is satisfied. In the capital city of Ottawa, conveniently located mere steps from the North Pole, literally everyone works for the government, so rush hour starts at 3:45 p.m. and maternity leave lasts for seven years.

From the third week of law school onward, Kristen's destiny was obvious. She could projectile vomit an entire un-masticated textbook at will. She levelled everyone with a cool disinterested stare and had an android manner of pronouncing the words "That wasn't in the reading." Kristen is beige. She drives a Honda Civic into the Canada Industrial Relations Board in Ottawa each morning, where she doesn't do a great deal of work – which is just fine, because none of it is very important.

Moving down the ladder: if Kristen was a dullard, Phillip was a grub. He spent most of his time grubbing around the Legal Clinic – a charity outfit staffed largely by students – reciting his favourite lines from *Law and Order*. Whenever one of the Clinic's hapless clients landed in the clink, Phillip would hang around like a bad smell in rolled-up shirtsleeves, wheezing, "I don't have time for that now. For the love of God, I have to get my client out of jail!" – a falsehood, as Phillip couldn't liberate anything except potato chips.

I entered law school in the wake of an undergraduate degree in "Business Management," which had taught me everything about businessmen except how to actually become one. I knew that businessmen fornicated with their secretaries in boardrooms of purest mahogany, and I'd learned about cost-management accounting and the art of the deal-maker, about managerial finance and being a risk-taker, about e-commerce schemes and following your dreams, about digital data management and standing out in a crowd and organizational behaviour and living out loud, but it increasingly seemed impossible to do all of these things at once; and besides, there were no job postings for "aspirant businessman, junior level." Law school seemed like a shrewd way to short-circuit the path from retail sales clerk to Board of Directors. Law was value for money; it was a Respectable Profession. It is a truth universally acknowledged that lawyers, though seldom beloved, are solid, serious blocks of society, and even the dullest ones have passable incomes.

The competition for law school, like the competition for literally anything that might ever actually lead to viable employment, was cutthroat. Fortunately my marks were excellent, in part because I had laced my degree with elective offal like "The Comic Book as the New Bildungsroman" and "The Female Motif in Japanese Graphic Novels," and also because I had cheated. Twice a term I'd paid a guy in Kolkata named Basu to synthesize two-thousand word essays on Maslow's theory of motivation or the effects of brand image on consumer buying preference, or once, for triple pay, on an elective, *Tartuffe* in credible French. Basu was a remarkable scholar. The Dean of Law was plying me with wine-and-cheese "student achievement" receptions months before I'd even graduated, and I smiled back with all my brightness, and called liberally upon my ability to nod convincingly and produce superficial natter on nearly any topic. In actuality I was an expert on precisely nothing except (a) H. Rat's Best Pub and Pizzeria and (b) the going rate for forgery in West Bengal.

In those first days at law school my gait alternated between a swagger and a skulk. I could almost smell the patent leather briefcase I would use to cart money around when I made partner at a flash law firm, but at the same time anxiety covered me like a rash. It was not the nervous itch of conscience; no, it was the paralyzing fear of a soldier who has somehow dropped his gun. The essays I'd commissioned from my man in Kolkata had greased me through my little patchwork quilt of a B.A., but law school was an infamously more difficult animal. At first Basu balked at my requests for quick-time short answers on civil procedure and three-thousand word essays on Canadian tort law, but he had a genuine academician's pride in my unblemished wall of A's, and he really enjoyed rupees. He agreed to ghostwrite my first year of law school in exchange for a dazzling sum, contract to be re-negotiated after two terms. I hung up the phone whistling *We are the Champions* and pranced to the post office to ship him a photocopied batch of first-year curriculum textbooks.

If someone had called me out at that very moment, I might have hesitated. It's one thing to plan the deed, another to execute it and something else entirely to nod one's head and affirm it: yes, I am a sham and a charlatan; yes, I am a cheat and a liar and a fake. Fortunately – or unfortunately, as it turned out in the long run – no one called me anything, and the plan went off without a hitch. With my scholarship secure and my little brown buddy Basu at the helm of the Good Ship Fraudulence, academic success seemed assured. The only drawback was that my little brown buddy Basu was deadly expensive. My rapidly accruing debt began to inspire aggravated panic attacks, but I found that I could soothe myself by meditating upon fleets of BMWs. When that failed I simply burned my loan statements.

I'd heard on some TV chat show that the *appearance* of being successful is an excellent predictor of actual success, so to cultivate the right *look* for a hotshot young lawyer on the make I swathed myself in leather, uniform of the moneyed and powerful: brown leather shoes, a top-grain leather satchel instead of a backpack, and a leather clipboard. I felt a head taller. In retrospect, I looked like a suitcase. To complete my new look I dispensed with my girlfriend Bianca, the Slovenian girl I'd been dating for eight or nine months. Bianca was dark-haired and short with a pretty, sulky smile. She was studying to be a hairdresser and her mother owned the laundromat where we'd first met, but she still saved her pennies to buy Gucci handbags. She'd been ecstatic over my admission to law school, and when she made a remark to the effect of "things are really starting to turn around for us now" after treating me to a celebratory dinner, an alarm bell started clanging in my brain. If Bianca thought she could ride around unchecked in my future BMW, gradually insinuating herself into my future executive-style penthouse with concierge service on Hazelton Avenue – well, she simply wasn't attractive enough for that. I told her that things just weren't working out anymore. She asked me what the hell I was talking about. I hung up.

With Bianca gone, I aimed high: I paid court to the queenly Michelle and her breathtaking golf jerseys. My suit was unsuccessful: after four weeks of lunch treats and free drinks, Michelle declared that I was "basically her gay best friend." Sexual access was never granted, but she did consent to work with me on three assignments for our Legal Ethics course, saving me a tidy packet of bribes to Basu in the process.

Life was good, a smooth trajectory of classes and lunches and booze-ups that would eventually terminate somewhere in a plush big city office. I was neatly skirting the system, and I will admit to the occasional twinge of conscience over it. The twinge escalated to something like sorrow whenever I caught sight of Phillip bent double over his Civil Law textbook, his fat-squashed eyes trained on the pages. Phillip, whose girth and slavering enthusiasm would certainly exclude him from the ranks of the champagne-and-cigars elite, knew as all of us did that no matter where you ranked in the social order, the marks you obtained in your first year of law school decided your entire career. He had no shot at the likes of Smith Johnson or Sullivan Phelps or the other multinational million-dollar turnover firms, but if he filed down his acne and managed a passable grade point average, he might just scrape his way into a mid-size employment law firm, where for the first four years of his career he would probably work over a hundred hours a week.

If law school was a contest, then the on-campus job interview was the prize. The real jackpot was a full-time job offer after graduation: the big firms rarely hired anyone who hadn't managed to bag a spot in the summer pools. The administrative apparatus at the university spent weeks grooming the school – and us – in anticipation of the great event. Tables were laid out, curtains were ironed, the great wooden banisters were rubbed down with spicy oils – all that was missing was the Dean flitting about with a basket of rose petals. A "career consultant" named Svetlana was called in to coax the slouching, snacking, compulsively text-messaging body of students, who pounced like starving animals onto any display of free food, into behaving like professionals. Svetlana applied makeup with the famed Eastern European light touch and held weekly seminars where she recounted anecdotes from the on-campus interviews of yore, rolling her blue-daubed eyes to the heavens like a Verdi heroine. When the appointed day came, a horde of lawyers, all clad in the same livery of dark suit and swagger, would descend on the west parking lot and fill it with impressive cars. They usually stood around the Great Hall guffawing for a few minutes, and then at length the lucky interviewees were summoned forth to answer a battery of questions that usually included "Why are you interested in a summer job at our firm?" and "Where would you like to be in five years?" The honest answers were "Because I need a job" and "Bermuda." The correct answers were "Because you're my favourite law firm in the whole entire world" and "Billing hundreds of hours a week as an associate at your firm." In short the on-campus interviews, provided one had the marks, the right spit and polish and just a touch of the hypocrite, were one's ticket to the big time. I could hardly wait.

And then my life exploded, because Basu died. His deadness destroyed my life. I received word of his death via a strange e-mail from Basu's own account: "BASU HAS PASSED ON. VERY SAD DAY FOR EVERYONE. THX,

GAJANANVIHARI." My first thought was that Basu was a crook. He was thin and soft-spoken in white T-shirts and had a pleasant, genteel-sounding Anglo-Indian accent, but that shark took me for every penny by constantly inventing new expenses: one day a reading premium, the next a pencil-sharpening fee. We'd video-chatted to discuss the midterm essays only two nights prior and despite the huge dark circles under his eyes from all of the studying he did at my behest, there was no coughing, no sputum, no cancerous bald head, no knife at his throat, nothing to indicate that death was imminent.

"The jurisprudence in this particular area is very tricky," he'd said. "I'll need a fifteen percent raise if I do this again."

"What do you mean *if*? We have a contract!" I'd hollered.

"What do you know about contracts? I wrote your entire Contracts take-home exam for you," he'd replied, and coolly hung up.

The strange e-mail from the detestable Gajananvihari followed shortly thereafter. Quaking a little inside with the premonitions that my academic pyramid scheme was about to collapse, that I had been neatly crooked out of a hefty deposit for an imminent five-thousand word paper for my Property Law course, and that my chances at the on-campus law firm interviews lay in ruins, I shot off a reply, but the e-mail bounced. I never heard from Basu again.

Maybe he cracked under the pressure of being my full-time academic avatar. Maybe he found a better gig and didn't know how to let me down. Maybe a rival plagiarist bumped him off and he really did kick the bucket. It didn't matter. If Basu wasn't biologically dead, he was dead to me, and I was too busy wringing my own neck to mourn him. There was no question of academic virtuosity at this point in my career: I was borderline illiterate. I repaired to the Internet and found a law student in Rajasthan named Priya with a lovely bright smile who promised forty-eight hour service and cut-price fees. She delivered the goods two hours before the deadline, beautifully typed and chock full of impressive footnotes, and for a few days I felt wonderful.

Then my Property Law professor summoned me to his office for a sinister *tête-à-tête* about my paper's strange colonial slang, as well as its suspicious volume of citations for the Supreme Court of India. He successfully ascertained from our conversation that not only had I neglected to write the paper, I actually hadn't read it. He ripped my essay into fifty pieces and frog-marched me to the Dean's office. I won't get into the sordid details of that terrible afternoon. Suffice it to say that I alternated between pleading insanity and begging for mercy, and by begging I mean that I actually sank to my knees at some point. In my supplicant's pose I even dripped some weepy snot onto the Dean's Persian-silk knotted carpet, a move which turned out to be my masterstroke. Eyeing the snot, she gave me a quick, disgusted parting lecture on ethics but – wonder of wonders – she declined to have me expelled. My punishment, she declared, would be an official warning in my file and the revocation of my scholarship. She also warned me – cool, disdainful, stone-faced – that if I ever did it again, I would be hanged. I thanked her profusely. She said she would thank me to leave.

As soon as it was over I ran to the gents' and splashed cold water all over my rank body. Then I cursed Priya to the skies. It was her fault, that Indian temptress with her white smile and bargain basement prices and shoddy-as-shit workmanship. I poured profanity all over her and her ancestors, but in my heart I knew that she wasn't to blame. It was Basu's fault, really. The dead bastard. At that moment I envied him.

I strode into Property Law class the next morning to a chorus of hissing and whispering and whipped-around heads. I took one look and I knew that my plight was now front-page gossip. I stood there in the lecture hall door for a good half a minute, seething at the forty-four smirking faces, and then the room went quiet. The world gleamed red for a moment, and in that dangerous moment of silence, I screamed "SHUT UP! ALL OF YOU JUST SHUT UP!" The backlash was instant. The wrath of a hundred righteous baby lawyers descended on my head. Thereafter the Kristens and Michelles and Blakes of the upper social strata stopped including me in invitations to trivia nights at The Devil's Advocate and post-exam wine-and-cheese soirées. Even Phillip eventually took the cue and slurped off in the other direction when I entered the student lounge. My grades plummeted.

The pyramid had crumbled at last. I was buggered.

The jig was up. My goose was cooked. If only Basu had lived. I never would have ever contemplated working for Octavian Castro.

Chapter 2
Octavian Castro

You may as well know that my name is Walter Roger, technically speaking. Professionally speaking, my name is mud. Octavian Castro, the secretive and close-mouthed, the architect of my destruction, still carries his reputation intact, clean and unspotted as his crisp designer shirts.

Everything about Octavian Castro was "classified." The man was opaque. He would glide around campus in his expensive clothes, his back unburdened by backpack and hands neatly folded to his chest. Outside of classes he was invisible: no Legal Clinic, no mock trial competitions, no post-exam booze-ups at The Devil's Advocate Pub. He looked skittish if you asked him about his family and deeply offended if you asked about his plans for the weekend. Pressed for answers, he would stroke his chin like Confucius and say, "That's classified information, I'm afraid." He was of medium height and thickness with an ambiguous olive skin: he might have been Syrian, Spaniard or Sikh. I eventually learned that his father was some kind of a Cuban diplomat and the family had flitted all over South America before landing on Colombia.

After we became better acquainted – Octavian never allowed that we were friends – I learned a few other things as well. For instance, Octavian's interest in practicing law was approximately nil. He'd been earmarked by his family for a prime sinecure at the international trade bureau in Bogotá, and had been bidden to spend a few years at a foreign law school to make the appointment credible. When Octavian refused, his uncle put a Sig Sauer pistol to his head. Two days later Octavian was on a plane to Toronto.

Octavian hated Canada. Most of us hated Canada by the time winter rolled around, but Octavian did it with flair and panache. Whereas I simply used drugs – highly illegal ones – to dull the winter cold and summer mould of my hovel of a basement apartment, Octavian rented a bungalow, painted the whole interior a glossy black and mounted a huge print of Goya's sick-inducing masterpiece *Saturn Devouring His Son* over his twelve-seat dining table. He spent most of his time in his boudoir, preening.

I knew Octavian by sight – he cut an unmistakeable tall figure in glistening Italian shoes – but we intersected for the first time some months after my sweaty interrogation at the Dean's office had reduced me to the social equivalent of syphilis. I didn't particularly miss the dumb buddy jock banter with Blake or the sexual frustration lunches with Michelle, but I was beginning to be annoyed by the pointed discussions of legal ethics that seemed to erupt apropos of nothing whenever I was in earshot. Lawyers have an exaggerated sense of other people's obligations. Let he who is without sin cast the first stone, said Jesus; well, these budding barristers must have all been spotless maidens and sinless knights-errant, with the passive-aggressive boulders they lobbed at my arse.

"The chicken curry tastes like it's been marinated in sweat," announced Blake one time when he was in front of me in line at the cafeteria. "Maybe the cook outsourced it to India. A lot of jerks seem to be doing that these days."

"Shut up, Blake."

"Some people are just out to exploit the third world for whatever they can get," explained Mohamed, talking over me.

Michelle, the lithe and golden-haired, cornered me once when I bumped into her at the gym.

"I'm disappointed in you, Walter," she said, eyes moist with her own morals. "I feel like you let me down. You lied to me."

"What do you mean, I lied to you? I never lied to you."

"You let me believe that you were something other than what you are. I want you to promise me to be true to yourself."

Handed down like the Wisdom of Solomon. Instead I said: "You are so right, pretty girl. Let's hang out tonight. What do you say?"

"No."

QQ

So I was shunned by everyone, but regrettably I wasn't invisible. Far from it: I was famous, and eyes followed me everywhere I went. Accounts of my crime had been enlarged to heroic proportions. That I was a serial plagiarist was common knowledge; the very freshest new gossip held that I was also a prostitute. The idea, as I heard it explained by a pair of whispering, bespectacled girls as I stood in the cafeteria coffee line one morning, was that I had secured my entrance scholarship by feigning homosexuality and servicing the extravagantly gay Constitutional Law professor Dr. Lannister, who chaired the admissions committee.

"And he actually swallowed it. Can you believe that?"

I tapped the taller one on the shoulder. "I know you're talking about me," I said. "Ever heard of slander?"

The girl looked at me with her magnified eyes like I was a stray hair in her supper. Then she said: "Please don't touch me."

"And don't touch me either," said the other one.

"And don't touch me neither," said Emma from behind the counter, and the cafeteria collectively guffawed. Emma was the Romanian immigrant who poured the coffee.

The transformation from golden boy to geisha boy was complete; I was a fallen man, and I ate my warmed-over pizza in the back of the cafeteria alone and always alone, in the extreme discomfort of one who is being watched.

Octavian, on the other hand, was a loner by choice. He had a small group of Gangnam-style exchange-student buddies from Hong Kong and they used to enjoy splitting bottles of home-distilled brandy, spectacularly illegal, in plain sight of everyone in the rather beautiful Gothic-style law library that was the pride of the university. The department was crawling with finks and rats – as if they cared one iota about spilled brandy on the *Immigration Law Cyclical and Periodical* – but the Dean's office wouldn't touch him. Foreign students were good value: they paid higher fees and lent credence to the amusing fiction that the university was an international hub for cosmopolitan scholars rather than a local hub of inbreeding.

We met formally over blackmail. Octavian beckoned me over to his corner one day in the library during exam season, enthroned like the Emperor Charlemagne on a big leather chair.

"How's your buddy Professor Lannister these days, Walter?" he said conversationally.

I ignored that. "Working hard, or hardly working, Octavian?" I spoke in an affected way in those days. It was my best guess at what a real lawyer was supposed to sound like: a massive prick.

"Neither. Have a seat, Walter Roger. I have some excellent news for you. We're partners for the Real Estate Law exam."

I'd forgotten about the Real Estate exam and its peculiar regulations. There were no tests, no essays or presentations: one's entire grade was determined by means of a final examination, to be completed in pairs over forty-eight hours. A good partner was tantamount to a free A+ and students campaigned hard to bag the likes of Mohamed and Blake and Michelle; when those were taken they even tussled over scraps like Marcella, who at the very least could be counted on to squeeze the answers out of someone smarter. For all his mystique and glamour, no one would touch Octavian, not even his jolly band of quasi-alcoholic Hong Kongers; his capacity for sloth was too well-known, and this was serious business, this was grades, this was a summer job at a glossy downtown firm and five years later it was an Audi and a luxury condominium.

I slumped down into the chair opposite him. "I completely forgot. We had to hand in a mock pre-trial conference report for Criminal and I pulled an all-nighter to get it done."

"The sign-up sheet was posted this morning. No one wanted to work with you."

I flared a little at that. "Apparently no one wanted to work with you either, Octavian. Isn't that why we're having this conversation?"

"Michelle asked to be my partner. I said 'no'."

"That wasn't very smart, buddy."

Octavian smiled endearingly in the kaleidoscope light that streamed down from the stained glass windows. "I wanted to work with you, the man who goes gay for an 'A'."

"For the love of God it wasn't like that —"

"The man who gets on his knees for his B's —"

"I NEVER GOT ON MY KNEES FOR —"

"Stop. The precise position you assumed doesn't matter now. The favours you did for Professor Lannister are impressive, but don't misread me, I'm not interested."

"I can't believe this. What do you want from me, Octavian?"

His white smile was unwavering between his soft-looking pink lips. "This isn't personal, Walter. It's purely professional. I want you to write the Real Estate Law exam. Alone. When you're finished, you can put my name on it. Above yours, I think, would be best."

I stared into my own reflection in Octavian's glossy laptop cover: bloodshot, with dry skin on my face sloughing off from sleeplessness and pot. "Octavian, why would you do this to me? What have I ever done to you? I don't even know you."

"Nothing. But I don't like exams. I'd prefer if someone else wrote them for me. This topic bores me."

"Are you joking, Octavian? I'm not writing your exam for you. If I took this to the Dean's office I could have you kicked out for academic dishonesty."

"What a hypocrite," marvelled Octavian, leaning in so close that I could smell his spicy shampoo. "I don't think you'll be reporting anything to the Dean's office, Walter. I happen to know that you avoid the place like the plague, and I think we both know why. Bought any good essays from India recently, you hooker?"

"Come on, Octavian," I whined. "Give me a break. If you're hoping for a free 'A' you've picked the wrong guy."

"I couldn't care less."

I was a mediocre chess player at best but I knew a checkmate when I saw one. I wrote the Real Estate exam alone in my basement, and when I finished it I signed two names across the front page in angry pencil. That was the conclusion of my first encounter with Octavian Castro.

ΩΩ

The afternoon after the Real Estate exams were handed back I spotted Octavian in the law library mounted on his usual leather armchair, flagrantly sipping brandy. He raised his eyes from his book and waved me over. I should have punched his head in, or at the very least refused him, but instead I trotted over like a trained pig.

"You're looking glum, chum," he said, his Spanish *r* rolling in caramel tones.

"Haven't you heard, Octavian?" I snarled at him. "We got a 'C' on the Real Estate exam. I bet you're real proud of yourself now, aren't you?"

"Oh that," said Octavian, drinking lightly from his tankard. "So what?"

"Is that crack in your glass, Octavian? I had an A-minus average last semester. This term I'm shooting straight C's and my average is shot to pieces. Who would ever hire me now? You?"

"I don't buy prostitutes, so no," he said.

I ignored that. "I was *this* close to a summer job at Sullivan Phelps. I shook hands with one of their partners after a criminal litigation moot. He said I had the right stuff for corporate litigation. Now I'll be lucky if I can get a job fighting parking tickets."

"Wow," said Octavian, looking at the ceiling.

"Do you know what the partner said to me? He said, 'Maybe I'll see you at the on-campus interviews'. I had it made, I'm telling you."

"Wow."

"I can't afford not to succeed," I said, and to keep the tears at bay I stared at my own reflection in Octavian's high-gloss shoes. "I'm serious, I can't afford it, I'm choking on my student loans. I don't even know how much I owe anymore. Look, don't believe everything you hear about me. It was complicated."

"Wow."

"Am I boring you or something, Octavian? This is all your fault."

"Yes, Walter, you are boring me," said Octavian, drinking brandy in tiny civilized sips. "When I heard you were outsourcing your papers to India, I thought you were quite a clever guy. I overestimated you, Walter Roger. Believe me, brother, you don't want to work at Sullivan Phelps. Sullivan may feed your body, but in the end Phelps cannot feed your soul. Every two weeks they will toss some of their spare change at you, and then what? Will you bark like a seal and buy yourself a rubber ball? This is not life. This is humiliation."

"So I want to work at Sullivan Phelps. So what? Is ambition a dirty word now? Are you and your little Asian friends too important to get jobs?"

"That, Walter Roger, is classified information. But let's just say that I want more out of life than to go prematurely bald debating contract punctuation. As for this dump" – he gestured at the library – "the notion that anyone should spend three years memorizing nineteenth century real estate law cases is absurd. This isn't Plato. This isn't Neruda. Lawyers don't sit around debating the philosophical merits of selling your house. They screw each other on technicalities to win and spend the rest of their time pouring alcohol into rich clients on the golf course. I know this because my father is one of them, amigo. You want to be a big shot? Go study golf full time."

We were sitting by the stained glass windows in the thick of law library traffic. Students and professors and stray lawyers were milling all around us, but Octavian didn't trouble himself to lower his voice. There was a click of high heels on polished wood and we both looked up to see Michelle tapping toward us, clutching a pallet of books adorably to her chest. "I was just talking to Lijun," she said to Octavian, all height and scholarly spectacles. "He told me you were up here."

"We're about to go and get some pizza," I said to the curve of her hips. "Octavian's treating. Want to join us? You look amazing today."

"We're doing nothing of the sort," said Octavian calmly. "I'm going to finish my drink and then I'll probably paint for a while."

"Paint? What, you're an artist now?"

"True artists create from a place of inner stillness."

"I love art," decided Michelle. "I should try painting some time."

"Try drawing first. Too many people paint without knowing how to draw. You can't master colour until you've mastered composition."

"Maybe you, Mr. Rembrandt, could give me a couple of lessons."

"Why not?" said Octavian, and they both looked at me like I was a staph infection.

"See you guys," I said as coolly as I could, and buggered off back to my apartment to get high.

♎

Octavian was a handsome bastard, I have to give him that much. He had a sort of invisible magnetism that seemed to pique the curiosity of law school's pyramid-tip dwellers. He was invited to everything, but attended nothing as far as I could discern and although he wasn't well-known around campus, he was well-liked nonetheless.

"Oh, I know Octavian, sure," someone would say agreeably. "He's a good guy."

"That Octavian is such a character," was the reply, usually from a girl. "He's always walking around with a poetry book."

It was true. He stalked morosely around campus carrying volumes of Pablo Neruda, but spent most of his time in the law library dawdling between classes, alternately poring over novels and concealing the contents of his laptop screen.

"Why would you assume I'm watching pornography?" said Octavian icily. "Pornography is degrading to women."

"Why the hell else would you snap your laptop shut whenever anyone comes within fifty paces of the library? You're jumpy as hell."

"The absence of evidence isn't evidence. Didn't your friend in India teach you that?"

He turned the computer around. There was a music video playing on the screen, a Latino boy band outfitted in matching bandanas.

"That's genuinely more embarrassing than pornography," I said.

"Really? How did Professor Lannister's semen taste?"

A mere few weeks prior, I'd had my pick of friends at law school. Now I mooched around the study carrels in the orbit of a raving, cantankerous sloth: a man who spent half his time sleeping and the other half dispensing casual insults. "Jesus, take it easy Octavian. I need to start my readings, anyway. I'm a week behind in Torts."

He swept me with an indifferent gaze and withdrew a book from under the desk.

"*Dead Souls*," I read. "By Nikolai Gogol."

"You'd like it. In fact, you're the title character." He tipped himself a shot of bootleg brandy under the desk. He didn't offer me a drop.

♃

Like a lovesick groupie, I took to waiting around for Octavian in the library or in the common room. He seemed to enjoy this. Or rather: I amused him. It wasn't quite friendship, but it was better than the odorous solitude of my basement. He tolerated me so long as I refrained from diatribes about Basu or the Property Law professor or the fickle friendships of Mohamed and Michelle, and he inevitably had an urgent appointment with a Russian novel whenever I started moaning about my ruined career. The rumours that swirled around me supplied him with material for his acidic comedy routines, but he had no interest in discussing them directly, and he certainly never exerted himself to disapprove of me. After some months he actually condescended to invite me to a Mediterranean dinner party in his famed bungalow with its shining ebony walls and two-metre-tall Goya prints. The meal gleamed with rich oils and vermillion spices, and the elegant, drunk Hong Kongers and three uptight Iranian engineering students who made up the rest of the party went into ecstasies praising it. Octavian, who wore chef's whites, wholeheartedly agreed with them. I parroted along with whatever they said, but the truth was that years of fast food fare had eroded my taste buds, and *mirza ghasemi* tasted much like a McMuffin.

The much-vaunted on-campus interviews came and went. I'd been nursing a wisp of hope that God was good, and would heap His blessings upon my forty-seven applications to the glossiest law firms in Toronto, Montréal and New York. I'd printed them on hundred-pound paper and bound them in morocco; if they weren't the best, they were certainly the densest. But my day was done. No doubt the chorus in the leaky Dean's office had brayed my tale to the world, but even if they hadn't, my piss-poor post-Basu grades stood out on my academic transcript like hairy warts on a supermodel.

I could tell you the rest of the story. I could produce a tome of details about how I groped my way through the rest of law school, but these are neither interesting nor pleasant for me to recount, so a précis will have to suffice. After fumbling my way solo through a battery of courses – Administrative Law, Advanced Litigation, Civil Procedure and all the rest of it – I finally started to get the gist of being a student, having spent five beer-sodden years merely impersonating one. By the end of it my powers of writing and reasoning had improved quite a bit, and I even learned how to mash statutes and case-law into something resembling legal reason, but it was too late, far too late. In retrospect I probably should have quit, declared bankruptcy and headed west to Alberta to work on the blistering hole known as the tar sands. There was good money on the drilling rigs in Fort McMurray, and about as much prestige as a two-bit parking-ticket lawyer. It's funny how one's brain locks onto something and then seizes up; at the time I had barricaded myself into a tunnel that could not possibly end anywhere except for a lawyer's office. The idea of a day's labour bashing stones until they coughed up some crude oil was as foreign as Mongolia.

After a time, the class gossip mill found something else to grind. Someone discovered that Cathy Bilyk, a forty-something mature second-year student who always wore a blue trench coat, was actually a bitterly divorced mother of three who had calculated that it was cheaper to become a lawyer than to continue paying one. The acrid details of her custody wars – her husband's teenage mistress, his secret family in upstate New York, her wads of cash stashed in a secret cavity in the family pet – were all online in the *Family Law Review and Circular*, and were soon being passed from hand to hand amid gasps and giggles. The buzz around me died. My old friends simply forgot I existed. I bumped into Mohamed outside the campus gym in the autumn of third year when all the leaves were turning to rust, and he squinted at me with his beanlike vegetarian gaze like he'd never laid eyes on me in his life.

I finished law school in a hot blaze of mediocrity. My final set of grades was poor-to-middling. I entered a contract writing competition and came in fourteenth. I participated solo in a mock trial competition and won the right to coffee and crudités afterwards.

The final tally after three years of law school:
One diploma, framed
Number of kilograms gained: four
Number of friends made: one-half, if you counted Octavian
Debt: astronomical
Number of job offers: zero.

Chapter 3
The Apprenticeship of Walter Roger

And that, dear readers, is how I ended up as an indentured serf in an office the size of a chickpea over an Indo-Pak restaurant called Zaika's Place in Mississauga. I tried to tart the place up a bit by getting a gavel embossed on the glass door and nailing up a sign proclaiming "Castro and Roger Professional Legal Corporation" to the world, but after a time I gave it up. The legal profession and the world's oldest profession have quite a bit in common: location, location, location. The loveliest courtesan on earth can't bill harem rates in an alley behind a Motel 6 – which is precisely where we were located. I nearly had to break Octavian's arm to get my name added to the sign.

"This is the most dismal location in the city, Walter. Our clients will be exclusively immigrant scum. If they see a Roger on the sign, they'll flee. Especially if you illustrate."

"If I said the words 'immigrant scum', you'd call the Human Rights Commission."

"Did you just say 'immigrant scum'? What a racist."

"*I'm* a racist? You won't let me put my name on our sign because it's too white."

"Yes. Just like your mom. Wait, she's not a racist. She'll clearly mate with anything."

"You're a pig, Octavian."

Octavian relented in the end. But it was the last battle I won.

I've skipped ahead a little bit. Nearly a year and a half had elapsed since graduation, which I'd celebrated by moving back into my childhood bedroom and swiftly devolving into adolescence. Within one week the nicely redone room with its new wicker furniture was polluted beyond recognition with pizza residue. I had even recaptured my teenage acne with all of its hues and textures. My mother, who'd been so proud of my admission to law school, filled the house with sighs.

I'd completed my legal apprenticeship ("articling" was the official word for it) at the only place that would have me, which was a little Bulgarian family law outfit in a strip mall in the sodden dregs of Scarborough. It had taken four solid months of searching to find a placement and when the obstinate phone finally jangled for an interview my mood was one of ecstasy: at long last I would be a lawyer, a real live lawyer with clients and lashings of money. My new employers had been cagey on the phone, twice asking me if I was an alcoholic and aggressive about paying my meagre salary in cash, but even so, for a few hours I tasted some of the warm September joy I'd known in those first golden weeks of law school, when I'd boozed with Blake and flirted with Michelle and decorated the high-rise corner office in my imagination with a prime model from Victoria's Secret. My mother, who had lately grown weary of the unemployed bum she had gestated, caught a little of my mood and surprised me with a homemade sponge cake.

My heart sank a little when I first located the strip mall in a scrubby blue-collar neighbourhood that was physically and spiritually miles away from the high-gloss hundred-storey towers of Bay Street. The strip mall was passable, with a Filipino supermarket anchoring one end and a hardware store at the other, but the firm itself was squashed between a payday loan shark and an "adult fun" store adorned with a super-sized poster of a hairless male chest.

Penkov Family Law Barristers and Solicitors was composed of two married lawyers from Sofia and two blonde female receptionists-slash-paralegals – one with a straw-coloured bob and the other with a false waterfall of platinum curls. The office itself was furnished with admirable taste and restraint, with Persian carpets in the lawyers' suites and framed Kandinsky prints behind the heavy oak reception desk. Every morning the blondes would curl their lips at me in greeting, but all other communication in that outfit was strictly in Russian, and as in most family law offices most of it was miserable. The Slavs with ruined families who passed through the place scarcely spoke to me at all, but sometimes I could hear them crying over their child support payments and custody agreements.

It quickly became apparent that the Penkovs had hired me because they needed a "paper bitch": a photocopying delivery drudge who would work for minimum wage. My other attraction was that I was the functional equivalent of a deaf-mute in that miniature Kremlin. I wasn't blind though, which was a shame as far as they were concerned; my unimpaired vision informed me quite plainly that the burbling rill of Cyrillic-only clients always paid cash. Every few weeks the male Penkov grudgingly yielded some of it to me, under the table and always a few bucks short.

I had a tiny cherry-wood desk in the receptionists' area upon which the female lawyer would periodically deposit stacks of paper bearing instructions like "3 COPIES BOUND, COVER PAGE BLUE." Within two weeks I had discovered the real *raison d'etre* of the legal system: to convert trees into duplicates. An appeal filing to the divisional court, for instance, required triplicate copies of four separate books: an appeal book and compendium, a factum, an evidence binder and a book of authorities. I grew to hate the dry rub of paper on my fingertips, the ozone fumes of a fresh stack.

I did other chores as well. Four days a week the Penkovs sent me out for lunch. As good parsimonious immigrants they never would have dreamed of wasting their hard-earned money on take-out slop, no, not when perfectly good and cheap sandwiches could be assembled by the articling student. Ms. Penkov would dispatch me to Yummy Market for black bread and tomatoes and slices of *balik* which I glued together with surprisingly hot Russian-style mustard at my desk and served with sour pickles. Her husband occasionally took *kvas* as well, a sticky black liquid made of fermented bread. She would check the receipts, which she hoarded for tax purposes, and occasionally she even reimbursed me.

My sandwiches must have been delicious, because after a time I was promoted with great fanfare to the exalted rank of typist. One morning, one of the bottle-blondes shoved a stack of court papers covered in red ink at me and told me to make the edits.

"What's this?"

"It's a statement of claim."

"Right."

"It's initiating process for a new lawsuit. Perhaps being lawyer not for you. What about bodybuilder?"

I ignored that. "But I don't have a computer here. How do they expect me to do this without a computer?"

She gave me a sulky look with no meaning behind it. She was merely sulking for pleasure. Nonetheless I was pleased. In law school you learn the philosophy of "peace, order and good government," the meaning of *habeas corpus* and that one cannot suck and blow with the same breath, but they never teach you how to actually sue somebody, or what to do if somebody sues you. It was my first glimpse at the innards of lawyering.

The next day I installed my personal laptop in the office, plucked the first document from the stack and started plonking away sausage-fingered at the keyboard.

"No! Not like that!"

It was His Excellency Herr Penkov. He had appeared from nowhere like a Russian mist.

"Don't you know anything?"

"I've never done this before, alright, Mr. Penkov?"

"No attitude, please. If there is one mistake – even one mistake – in that Statement of Claim, the court clerk will throw it into the garbage and my clients will pay the price for your stupidity." He walked into his office and withdrew a thick book from one of the shelves.

"There."

"Thanks."

"It's the *Annual Practice*. Have you read it?"

"Sure."

"Sure," he said scornfully, and swivelling neatly on his heel he returned to his office and shut the door.

Of course I'd never read the *Annual Practice*. It was two

thousand pages long and almost completely bereft of sex scenes. After a few hours of excruciating perusal I deduced that it was basically a lawyer's instruction manual: how to serve a claim, how many days one had to respond to a lawsuit, the correct papers to file to defer a hearing, the required number of copies of a defence to file at the courthouse, and so on and so forth. Slowly, painfully, I set about re-typing the Statement of Claim according to the rules of the court. It took three hours hunched over the *Annual Practice* at the cherry-wood desk for me to complete it, but I was contented, even happy: I'd drafted my first legal document. By the ninth I was suicidal, especially after I learned that at really posh law firms, a lawyer was strictly a brainworker and would never have sullied himself by actually formatting a document for court. But I suppose it was a step up from cooking.

My most disagreeable duty by far was running the finished papers to the courthouse downtown. I would have happily sat all day in my shirtsleeves and slung-back tie creating sandwich art for the Bulgarian masses, if I might have been spared the perfidy of the court clerk's queue. The courthouse was on the ninth floor of a concrete block building whose sharp angles belied the zoological chaos within. Scores of runners, paralegals and lawyers clutching sheaves of paper were jammed together in a hot, angry conga line that wound its way up to a row of court clerks behind glass windows. The function of the court clerk was to reject your document on any pretext. Missing signatures and missed deadlines were fair forfeit, but heaven forbid that a judge's eyes might be polluted by a missing back-cover page or an evidence binder with a right margin three-fourths of an inch too wide. I once spent ninety minutes breathing in the angry sweat of the other hundred coolies in line, only to have my Statement of Defence rejected because we had missed the filing deadline by six and a half hours. Afterwards, it was back to the Penkovs' for a grade-A bollocking by the Tsarina Penkov, who excoriated me for wasting their time and money, then wordlessly pointed to my desk. I was on sandwich duty for the next three days.

On the day that Natalya Penkov handed me her dry cleaning and told me to have it back by five, I finally rebelled.

"Sure, Ms. Penkov."

"And tell them to take pins out this time."

"Can I come with you to family court today, Ms. Penkov?"

"You?" said the Putinesque female, widening her heavy-lidded blue eyes. "But you have no knowledge, no experience."

"That's because you and your husband refuse to teach me anything. The whole point of articling is for you to teach me how to be a lawyer."

"I am not your nanny nursemaid," she said, and with a touch to the tip of my nose with a French-manicured nail, she picked up her briefcase and left.

But I was unstoppable that day. I'd run out of weed money three days earlier and I hadn't quite managed to achieve my usual state of woozy compliance. I strode boldly to the lawyers' suite and stood at the door with my legs apart.

"Mr. Penkov."

The male lawyer spoke neat, precise English with only the hint of a Russian chill in it. He even sat precisely in his white shirt and plum-coloured tie.

"Be so good as to knock next time, Walter."

"Could I help you draft the Podolsky claim, sir? Not just type it this time?"

He raised his eyes, which sat blue-grey and even under a straight fringe of blond hair.

"You have been working here for six months. Suddenly you want to join the profession."

"I'll never get a job anywhere if you and your wife don't give me some real training, Mr. Penkov."

"I found four errors in your rendition of the Molckovsky application. You misquoted the *Family Law Act*. You make reference to the couple's two children, when in fact there are three. You omitted the entire final section. Finally, you have by some miracle cut an obvious link to an Internet pornography site and pasted it into the middle of the custody arrangement.

The wife's lawyer would have skewered us. When will you understand that there is no room for error? You are dealing with other people's children, with other people's lives."

I took this for fatherly encouragement and gave him the most boyish smile I could achieve, peeping up at him from under my eyelids. "I'm trying so hard, sir. I'm really learning. You've taught me so much."

"Flirting with me doesn't help your cause."

I tried a bit of cinematic boldness. "Come on, Mr. P. You know you love me."

"Then bend over."

He said it grey-eyed without flinching. Thus ended my uprising.

♎

By the end of my articling stint at the Penkovs', even Tsar Nikolas had to admit that I could photocopy an Affidavit of Service form with greater than average competence. Ms. Penkov relented ever so slightly and allowed me to carry her briefcase to the occasional hearing, but I was prohibited from speaking in the vicinity of the courthouse, and never to a client. The two flaxen-haired witches continued indifferent. I would have been better off at McDonald's. At least they had an employee meal plan.

At the conclusion of the articling period, the mentoring lawyer either had to hire you as an associate or give you the sack. On the last morning of my indentured servitude, Her Ladyship gave me a shopping list before leaving for a mediation session. At lunchtime I brought Mr. Penkov a bottle of *kvas*.

"Most kind," he said, and handing me his empty lunch plate he began to robe up for appellate court. I took the plate and watched him clothe himself.

"Does watching me undress give you sexual pleasure, Walter?"

"No."

"Are you quite certain? Perhaps I should start again. I like my employees to enjoy themselves."

"No. I mean yes, I'm certain. Jesus."

"Then kindly remove yourself and please finish the copying for the Bittner file. That hearing is coming up."

"It's the last day of my articling period, sir."

"Fine."

"Will you be hiring me back, Mr. Penkov?"

He snorted. "No."

I felt my face grow hot. "Is that all? No? I've worked for you for ten months. Don't you think you owe me more than 'No'?"

He fastened his white neck tab and shut down his computer. "Your generation thinks the world owes you everything."

"I swear to you I gave this job everything I had. Did you ever give me a chance, Nikolas? You know I have credit card people breathing down my neck but half the time you didn't even pay me on time," I said angrily.

"And you sound like a talent show contestant. Your generation believes that you should be rewarded for any expenditure of effort, no matter how pathetic. At your age I was a man. I was picking scrapyards over for spare parts in the evenings, I had a kid on the way and we needed money. I know what you've been doing all day; do you think we don't have Internet browser history in Bulgaria? You've been a subpar articling student and you will certainly be a subpar lawyer. I feel sorry for your clients, most of whom you will probably send to jail through your bungling. Leave your key with Valenka, please. Tell her to give you forty dollars to cover expenses. Good luck to you, Walter."

On my way out I nicked the mustard.

♉

And so that was that. I bid goodbye to the pink metrosexual on the "adult fun" poster, achieved a final parting leer from one of the clients of Money Mart and boarded the 86 Westbound bus for the last time. I was unemployed again, but more significantly, I was buggered. The one perk of articling was that one was still technically classified as a student, and students could cheerfully ignore student loans. The instant one ceased to be a student, interest began to accrue at a frightening rate. Six months later a bill would crash down like a knockout punch.

My mother met me at the door. She was still wearing her blue work blazer, so she must have sprinted to the bus seconds after quitting time.

"They fired you, didn't they."

"I just got home. I haven't even taken off my suit jacket yet."

"You and your jacket. Most people would get a good job first, then buy the fancy-dancy jacket. Not you. You do everything back-asswards."

"Okay. Goddamn you, jacket. If only I didn't have you we'd be rolling in cash. Let's go burn it."

"I've worked at the post office for twenty-two years. I started right at the bottom and worked my way up. I knew that as long as I kept my head down and did as I was told, my job would be safe."

"Your generation thinks the world owes you everything."

"What are you talking about?"

"What's for dinner?"

"I'm tired of being your maid. Make dinner yourself."

"You're my mother. You're supposed to take care of me. Oprah even said."

"You're a grown man, Walter. Maybe it's time you took a tiny bit of care of me. I know these immigrant types. If you'd kept your nose clean and showed Boris and Natasha you could work hard, you would have a job today."

"His name was Nikolas."

"I couldn't care less what his name was!"

Dinner that night was a mustard sandwich.

ꭅꭅ

After my stint at Bond Villains Barristers and Solicitors I locked myself in my bedroom for three months and killed myself. I should have, anyway. Who apart from his loyal dealer of cannabis and bottle narcotics would have mourned for Walter Roger? I sent a couple of e-mails to my old university friends, the ones I'd dumped when law school beckoned bright. Mike was living with a girl. Patrick had moved to Kingston. When neither of them expressed much interest in meeting me for a beer, I knew that I was still in love with my ex-girlfriend Bianca. Ah, Bianca. Her house smelled of root vegetables. Her mother ceaselessly did laundry. Clearly she was the only girl I'd ever loved. I'd been so desperately celibate over the past year that the mother would also have done nicely. I thought tenderly of Bianca with the dark lips that always said angry things to me, of the lovely shining dark hair that always smelled of strawberries, and dialled.

"Bianca."

"Yes?"

"I love you, baby. I don't know why I let you go."

"Walter?"

"Yo."

There was a long pause.

"You're high."

"High on my love for you, Bianca. I swear to God."

"OK Walter. Then prove it. Let's get married."

I hung up.

ꭅꭅ

After a time, life acquired rhythm. I rose at noon. From noon to one I attended to an array of pressing biological imperatives which need not be named. By one I was functional and ready for the day's computing. To save time, I turned on the computer immediately before boiling the water for my coffee. From 2 p.m. until midnight I applied myself to the Internet, with a short break at four to forage for food and another at six-thirty to fight with my mother. At midnight I tapped some weed into my vapourizer and puffed myself to sleep, and in the morning the cycle began again.

Three months of lurking on the Internet had convinced me that humans were the vilest species in existence. Anything that could feasibly have been inserted into a woman apparently had been. Then the news: if a child becomes a soldier in the middle of the Congo and no one is around to hear it, what the hell can I possibly do about it? What else? I read online forums covered in hate. I could map the entire anatomy of several famous actresses and I knew exactly which one had appeared nude in what films, and when, and exactly how empowering she had found it. I had played Minecraft until my eyes bled. I had window-shopped, virtually, for my top three supercars. It brought tears to my eyes when I considered the very real possibility that now I might never possess even one.

It was my mother's custom to burst in every evening after work and yip.

"Looking for a job?"

Swiftly close browser. "What else would I be doing, okay?"

"Well, you can stop. I've found you a job, Walter."

"Where?"

"At the post office."

"The post office has lawyers?"

"Probably. But what they want is a mail carrier. Rosa told me."

"You want me to be a mailman?"

"It's better than being a bum."

"Mom, I did not go to school for seven years so that I could end up as Postman Pat."

"Mail carriers make a good wage, they have great benefits and they get lots of exercise. You need to exercise. Look how out of shape you've gotten already."

"It's not my fault I can't afford a gym membership."

"Gym membership. What is wrong with you, Walter? At your age you have no excuse to sit inside all day. Why don't you go for a run? That's free."

"Mom, please could you leave me alone?"

"I'm sick of this, Walter. If you don't find a job within two weeks I swear I'll find you one myself. I don't want to kick you out but I can't watch my son throw away his life like this. Now get out of bed and help me make the salad."

I glared at her.

"Now!"

The day after this exchange, I woke at ten, rolled over, booted up the computer and started looking for a job. I applied to about thirty legal outfits in the greater Toronto area: real estate firms, corporate firms, sole proprietors, family lawyers. I was neither accepted nor rejected; I was simply nothing and I produced no effect. Dozens of letters pleading my virtues to employers all over the city disappeared into the web, a mere waste of electrons. After some time I edged away from the stricture of litigation positions and started applying for non-legal paper-shuffle positions in insurance firms and pharmaceutical companies. I had a single brief interview at a life insurance firm for what turned out to be a position in commission-only sales. I didn't get the job.

Six months to the day after I ceased to be a student, my mother shoved an envelope from the student loan demons under my bedroom door. I shredded the contents to dust in my hands and cut a little of it into my marijuana leaves; that night I smoked it. In my delirium I imagined that I was sending a signal to the world. *SOS. I've fallen and I can't get up.*

A couple of weeks later I was in the kitchen pouring myself a bowl of cereal when my mother burst through the door in a white gust of snow, hatted and coated with the mail in her gloves.

"Put some strawberries in that," she said immediately to the cereal. "You're not getting enough Vitamin D."

"*Alright*, Mom."

"There's another letter for you. I think it's another one of your student loan lett –"

I seized it, lit the stove, and made the envelope disappear into a hot ball of gas. Just before the contents incinerated I glimpsed the endless parade of digits owing to my lenders and my chest hurt so much I wanted to bury my face in the smoke until I blacked out. The paper began to char. My mother damped the bonfire by tipping the snow from her hat and gloves onto it, but to her credit she remained shriekless.

"Oh honey. That's a lot of money. What did you spend it on?"

"Nothing," I said dully.

"I can't help you, honey. Not for that amount, not for a tenth of that amount. Let me call Rosa for you. They're looking for mail carriers at the post office."

I was on the cusp of postmanhood. How much sweeter my life might have been had I kissed my loving mother and bid her to call Rosa, giver of jobs. But it was never to be: out of a clear blue sky Octavian called me the next day, and two weeks later, the "Castro and Roger Professional Legal Corporation," least successful law firm of all time, came sputtering to life.

Chapter 4
The Castro and Roger Professional Legal Corporation

The office over the Zaika restaurant was hot in the winter and a barbecued hell in the summer. Irritable South Asian immigrants poured their sweat into a roasting fire directly beneath us for nine hours a day, resentfully turning chunks of lamb and goat as they wondered why in the hell they had ever come to this country in the first place. The odours of goat korma and saag paneer wafted up through the stairwell at all hours, with the effect that I was permanently salivating.

Octavian and I each had tiny rooms of our own – Tinkerbell-sized spaces that could just accommodate a desk and chair – but we spent most of our time in the front waiting area, where we'd installed a ceiling fan to drive food smells away.

"Do you know anything about termination pay rules in the *Employment Act*?" I swivelled around to look at Octavian.

Octavian barely flicked his gaze up from his laptop. "No."

Of course he didn't know. Why should he? As a decorator he was a marvel: he'd installed a stylish golden sofa and applied a shiny varnish to the frames of our diplomas. As a lawyer he was useless. I knew now why he'd hired me: it was the Real Estate exam all over again. What I didn't understand was why he was skimming me for chump change in Toronto when there was a prize-plum job waiting for him back in Bogotá.

"Octavian."

"I'm a very busy man, Walter."

"No, you're a huge anus and you're driving me insane. I just did the accounts and we're bleeding money on this place. Can you tell me what the point of the Castro and Roger Professional Legal Corporation is? Are we a front for drug-runners in Los Urabeños? I have a right to know."

Octavian gave me a slow clap. "Los Urabeños, Walter. I'm impressed. Have you been going to night school?" His eyes dropped again. "If so, I must ask you to stop. Time is money.

As it happens, I sold my stake in the cocaine cartel last year. Satisfied?"

"They seriously issue shares?"

"Absolutely, amigo, and dividends too. If you were a good lawyer you would ask me to deny everything in writing. Fortunately you are not a very good one, and will probably stay in my employ forever."

"The second I've paid my student loan I'm out of here. I'm serious, Octavian."

Octavian donned headphones. "I look forward to many happy decades together."

♋

Our routine seldom varied. Octavian spent most mornings in secret communion with his computer. In the afternoons he made loud inscrutable phone calls to Miami and watched Spanish music videos on a carpet in his room, sometimes accompanied by Marycarmen, the new secretary, sometimes not. As for me, I did all of the grunt work I'd resented so bitterly at the Penkovs' and more: I drafted applications and motions, I chased down bills, I sent Marycarmen off to serve affidavits whenever she wasn't noisily engulfing Octavian.

As a real live lawyer in what was nominally my own practice, I could now litigate my little heart out, if only a judge didn't barbecue it first. Oh, how well I had come to know the judge's shrivelling lip. On television judges sat on the bench like sour milk while the lawyers hammed it up in couture for the camera in the gallery. Oh, the bollocking I got when I tried lines like "I object, Your Honour! I object!" and "With all due respect, Your Honour, opposing counsel is a liar!" on the fifty-something female judge in fashionable eyeglasses at small claims court. "I suggest, Counsel, that you have a hard look at the Rules of Professional Conduct," she said acidly. "It's called 'Conduct unbecoming a lawyer'. As for you, madam —" she addressed my client, "whatever you are paying this gentleman, it is too much."

With performance reviews like that, you might ask how we contrived to have any clients at all. That is an excellent query and here is your answer: we were dirt cheap. I mean that quite literally. After expenses, our hourly rate usually ended up roughly commensurate with the price of a bag of soil. This low-cost approach ought to have been vastly more successful than it actually was: don't we all detest those nasty grasping lawyers? Quick, why won't a snake bite a lawyer? *Professional courtesy!* My lawyer didn't want to marry his wife for her money. *But there was no other way to get it!* Har, har, har. In reality, the lawyer's office is one of the few stops on the desert of existence where the normal economics of supply and demand fail, because the act of hiring a lawyer is a triumph of psychology over logic: would you hire a lawyer shod in a T-shirt, offering buy-one-get-one-free divorces from behind a cubicle? Of course you wouldn't. You want your lawyer to look lawyerlike in a sharp suit behind a massive intimidation desk, and moreover you will pay top dollar for the privilege.

As Octavian had predicted, hardscrabble immigrants made up the bulk of our clientele, and every two weeks after paying the bills we divided the spoils like jackals licking at a very small rat. How I envied the postman, who sang so tunelessly as he carried our mail up the stairs. Good honest work! Fresh air and exercise, a pension, a disability plan and all that lovely money! Once when things were desolate I called my mother and asked her if Rosa still had a hot tip on a mail carrier. "Why honey, do you have a friend who needs a job?" she said.

"Can you just ask if it's available?"

"Sure, honey. I got so sick and tired of Rosa going on about her son's landscaping business. 'You know my handsome son?' I said to her. 'He's a successful lawyer now. Put that in your pipe and smoke it'. That's what I said."

I am no model of filial piety, but I was not yet prepared to inflict the loss of a successful lawyer son on my long-suffering mother. I said "Thanks, Mom" and shrank away to chase down an overdue bill from the local Brampton slumlord.

The secretary was a constant source of tension between us. Octavian simply hired whichever Latina beach babe he happened to be dating at the time – they all looked like sex dolls, with that open-mouthed strangeness – whereas I harboured the notion that a secretary ought to occasionally do some secretarial work. After a two-month wonderfully legal "trial period," he would fire her without consequence – if she hadn't quit already in a jealous rage. The last secretary had been a fabulously blasé Brazilian girl named Patrícia who rolled her eyes at everything I said, even banalities like "Could you please place a call to the court registrar's office?" Octavian had adored her.

Marycarmen, the secretary *du jour*, was a part-time nursing student who was just five feet tall with enormous, almost cartoonish black-rimmed eyes. At first I was envious of her lithe, perfumed, female omnipresence and then I was merely annoyed by the fact that it was impossible to coax her into doing any actual work. She was bored by most things that weren't Octavian, and perpetually terrified that her fanatically Catholic mother would locate her in his embrace and disown her for being both unchaste and an apostate. Today was no exception: when I returned to the office after a long morning screaming at the court clerk, Marycarmen popped panting out of our supply closet.

"Ay! I thought you were my parents. See you later, *mi amor*," she squeaked, buttoning herself, and blowing a kiss to the air she tripped down the stairs.

Octavian emerged stoop-shouldered from the tiny closet.

"How did you even fit in there?" I asked him.

"She's not that small. If you had any knowledge of fine international women, you would know that she's pretty average for a Mexicali girl."

"I meant the closet!"

Octavian stretched lazily and winked. "We might have to call in a repairman, brother. I don't know if these old floorboards can physically hold all the money we're raking in. Did you see the e-mail from Mr. Correa?"

"Yes. Will you answer it?"

"Definitely not. I'm busy."

"Busy doing what exactly?" I exploded. "I've got two applications to draft by Thursday. And who's handling the settlement conference on Friday? You?"

Octavian thought about it. "No."

I slammed down my notebook and lunged at him, twisting his arms around until I had him gurgling in a choke-hold. Octavian hefted me onto his back, pinching a spot just beneath my spine that shot pain directly into my temples. I screamed like a colicky infant while he freed himself, which was fine by me. I didn't much enjoy his cold neck-sweat on my lips.

"So violent," said Octavian mildly, settling back onto the little gold sofa and fanning at the aromatic fog of stewed goat that was Zaika's Thursday lunch special. "If you were black they would have locked you up a long time ago."

"So sue me for battery, Octavian. That way at least one of us will make some money off this place. I could barely make my credit card payments last month."

"Oh crap," said Octavian to his phone, before Marycarmen's perfume had even evaporated. "It's that girl Yamaira. I forgot I told her we'd have lunch today, but I'm seeing Marycarmen."

"Octavian, please," I said tiredly. "Marycarmen is supposed to be our secretary. How will we get anything done around here if you keep disappearing to mount her? I need help with the Benitez file."

Too late: Octavian was already pimpifying himself in the coat closet mirror, preening the lapels of a cream-coloured blazer. It was a perfect fit, absolutely skin-tight to the shoulders.

"You bastard, where the hell do you think you're going?" I said, but my curiosity got the better of me. "Who's Yamaira?"

"Classified," he said with his maddening Cheshire smile, and vanished down the stairs into the free world.

Chapter 5
Ferdinand Magellan and the Giant Loophole

When Octavian returned to the office several hours later, I was still stumped on the Benitez immigration file, and now to add to my woes Marycarmen was stretched on a chair in clinging leopard print eating a bag of Swiss chocolates – *my* Swiss chocolates – to great theatrical effect.

"Those are good, aren't they?" I said, watching the glide of her feline tongue. "Also, they were really expensive. By the way, thanks a lot for forgetting to serve that consent letter on the shopping mall file. You cost our client a thousand dollars and when he gets back from Ecuador he'll probably beat me to death."

Marycarmen flicked her big Telenovela eyes at me. "I know. These chocolates are the best. Want one, Octavian?"

"I could go for something sweet," said Octavian smoothly, with a significant glance at me that meant I should disappear.

I wished viruses upon them both, both electronic and biological, then I locked my door and called Ferdinand Magellan. Mags had been two years ahead of me at law school and we'd chatted at pub nights and seminars before I'd moved on to higher things like drug addiction. Mags was the best lawyer I knew. He was respectful to professors and gentle to hobos. He served faithfully in the Naval Reserve. He also had dim little blue eyes full of crumbly yellow bits and a peculiar lopsided gait that was the remnant of absolutely no childhood ailment at all – he just walked like a gimp. Thousand-dollar Italian suits died when Mags wore them, withering almost instantly into malodorous rags. I'm lying, of course. Mags was a pauper. He couldn't afford a single trouser leg of a thousand-dollar suit. His suits were all remnants from the Giant Tiger bargain rack, and occasionally his jacket and trousers matched. Mags, in case it isn't blindingly apparent, was too ugly for Bay Street. Instead he worked part-time at the Legal Aid clinic in Parkdale, where he squandered his talent on landlord and tenant squabbles. Three nights a week he moonlit as a legal dogsbody for a juice bottling company, sorting out permits and immigration papers for the South Asian wage slaves who constantly hit him up for small loans.

"Mags," I said.

"What is it now, Walter?" came the voice of Mags over the receiver. "Why can't you all just leave me in peace? Blake called me up the other day, do you remember him, he's such a prick. He wanted my advice on some of the regulations on the *Securities Act.* How should I know, I told him. I work at Parkdale Legal Aid, I said. Do you think the homeless queue up here for stock options?"

"Did you help him?"

"I had to get him off my back somehow. Bastard."

"You realize you could have billed him for it. He works for Sullivan Phelps, what difference does it make to him? He has a fat expense account."

"How could I possibly bring that up in the middle of conversation?"

"It wasn't a social call, stupid. He was using you."

"Is there a point to this phone call, Walter?"

"I need some help. It's an immigration matter. I'm desperate. And I have to be in court at three."

"Fine, but I'm counting this in my billable hours. I don't have time right now and I'm sick of taking phone calls from you idiots. Drop by my place later. After eight; the kids should be asleep by then. You'll find me a lot more willing if you bring beer."

Mags hung up and I breathed more easily. Mags' competence was matchless and lawyering was his *grande passion.* He read federal statutes for pleasure. He owned a framed print of Hammurabi's Code. He had invented no fewer than three tax loopholes.

My brief period of peace was pierced by the premonitory clouds of lilac perfume that meant Marycarmen was about to knock at my door. Her little face peeped into my office with those big stupid doe eyes I took such pains to avoid staring into.

"Hi Walter."

"Hi Marycarmen."

She stood there looking at me. I tried again. "So, uh, how's nursing school? Is there lots of blood and stuff?"

"Do you know where Octavian went? He said he had to go."

Covering for Octavian was another of my duties. "Uh, right, he had a pre-trial conference. Could you possibly make those calls we talked about last week?"

She frowned. "He told me he was serving an assofdavid or something."

"Affidavit. OK, that's what he's doing then."

"Walter?"

"What?"

"I know Octavian's cheating on me. You don't have to cover for him. I was about to break up with him anyway."

Oh crap. "Look Marycarmen, Octavian loves you very much and – you know what, why don't you work it out with him when he gets back?"

"Do you want to be my boyfriend?"

"*What?*"

She gave me a coy look. Her eyelids were rimmed with a silver polish of some kind and she'd loosened her leopard coat a little to reveal a breathtakingly tight purple mini-dress underneath. I swallowed.

"Don't you think I'm pretty?" she said.

"Of course I think you're pretty – Jesus, what is this, Marycarmen, a trick?"

"Of course not," she said. "I think you're cute. I like you because you're always so sweet to me. Some guys, you just can't trust. I can really talk to you, Walter."

I think you're cute injected itself into my prefrontal cortex and instantly paralyzed my brain. I was now an idiot at the molecular level. "Well, this is all very flattering, Marycarmen, and I like you too, but – but what about Octavian?" I stammered.

She flipped her hair, sending another intoxicating cloud in my direction. "He won't care. I know he's seeing someone else anyway. Isn't he?"

"I guess, but –"

"See? I told you. So you're my boyfriend from now on. Okay?"

"Okay," I managed, my head swimming.

She leaned over, exposing a significant portion of her spectacular bosom, and gave me a lingering kiss on the cheek. "Bye, *guapo*."

"Bye, Marycarmen."

♋♋

I left for Mags' apartment on Bathurst straight from the courthouse, simultaneously pondering the meaning of Marycarmen, fidgeting with the phone for imaginary new e-mails, and losing at Star Poker. Mags answered the door with a beer in hand. He was wearing a T-shirt that read *Dinosaurs Live at the Ontario Science Centre! PARENT VOLUNTEER* and probably dated from the Mesozoic era. "What is that, a new smartphone?" he asked. "On one hand you whine incessantly about your debt. Then you go out and buy yourself a phone that's worth more on the open market than all of your organs combined. My three-year-old has more financial sense than you do."

"I need this phone," I said defensively. "It has all the games I like pre-loaded."

Mags snorted. Then he handed me the beer. He couldn't help himself. Mags was Mr. Nice Guy with a short fuse, a combination that seldom leads to anything good in our profession.

I sat down at his bleak little dining room table with congealed macaroni paste and a baby bottle on it. Over the table was a framed photograph of Mags next to an athletic-looking curly redhead with a pretty smile. "Where's the wife?" I said.

"'The wife'? What is this, the 1970s? Are you trying to be ironic or something?"

"Fine. How is your wife, the esteemed Mrs. Ferdinand Magellan?"

"I don't know. With her grandparents probably. She left the kids with me."

"That's rough. I'm sorry, Mags."

"Yup. I've lost all hope at this point. How's the practice?"

"I had a bummer of a day in court. Opposing counsel won the day by lying outright. Immoral prick. Have you met our new secretary, by the way? She's my girlfriend now. I think."

"Get real, Walter. Immoral. What does law have to do with morality?" said Mags, closing his eyes. "The French word for lawyer is *avocat*. A good lawyer is a good advocate for his client, and that is all. Leave morality to the judge."

"Judge this for me then. I've got a client with a niece on a student visa. She wants to stay in the country. Possible or not?"

"How should I know, as you've given me zero useful information?"

I shrugged. "Her uncle says she's so ugly that no one back home in Ecuador will marry her. Is there a pity visa or something?"

"If she's a grad student, get her a post-graduate work permit. Do it tomorrow, there's only a limited window for it before she graduates. Then get someone to make her a job offer."

"What if she can't get a job?"

Mags gulped his beer. "I didn't say she had to get a job. I said she had to get a job offer. Do you get my drift?"

"You're a genius."

At that he grinned at me with beery affection. "So have you got a girlfriend or what?"

"I honestly don't know."

He nodded again, sending a few flakes of dandruff tumbling onto his shoulder. "Love. It's just one giant mind game. Do you know how much further ahead I'd be in life if I'd been chemically castrated at thirteen? I think about it sometimes."

"You know what, Mags? I don't."

"So who is she?"

"Her name is Marycarmen. She's perfect in every way, except she's Octavian's ex. Should I be worried?"

"How long have they been broken up?"

"About an hour."

Mags took another sloppy gulp of beer. "As long as you're happy."

"I'm broke, I'm in debt and the entire bench of the Ontario Superior Court despises me. I don't want to talk about it, Mags. Just give me more alcohol. It's different for you. You actually like this stuff. You're good at it. Look how you solved my immigration problem."

He waved me away. "That was nothing. You want to see a real immigration scam? Read the *Canadian Naval War Act*," he said. "There's a loophole in it the size of your head." He grinned bug-eyed at me until I took the bait.

"Fine. What's the loophole?"

"I was reading some old military law a few days ago. According to the *Canadian Naval War Act, R.S. 1937*, any ship may be classified as military so long as it was registered in a Commonwealth country to a citizen in good standing and has at least one active member of the Canadian military on it. The law was enacted during the Second World War when a bunch of Maritimers volunteered their old schooners as laundry boats. It's obvious to me that someone just forgot to repeal it, but no one ever did. There's even some post-war jurisprudence supporting it. *Collins. v. R., Nova Scotia Supreme Court 1964*. Collins was a retired vice-admiral with a house in Florida and he wanted to get the Canadian government to green-light him over the American border as a military ship. Collins won his case. I read an archived interview with him in a 1965 edition of the Halifax *Dispatch* and apparently two cases of Screech were riding on the outcome. Are you starting to get the drift?"

"I don't know what the hell you're talking about, Mags. No one ever does."

"That's because you haven't read the *Citizenship and Immigration Act, R.S. 1994*. In fact, you haven't even skimmed it. I know this because your client's niece-and-visa problem was so trivial I'm actually almost embarrassed for you."

"If I wasn't drunk as hell, I'd be offended."

Mags clinked cans with me and resumed his monologue. "As you know, Walter, Canada is one of only two first-world nations on earth to espouse the principle of *jus soli*, or citizenship by birthright. The other country is the United States, but they closed pretty much all of their immigration loopholes after the Bay of Pigs. Of course, you could always snag your kid some *jus soli* citizenship action if you managed to squirt it out in Peru or Lesotho, but there aren't too many takers these days. So that's it. What do you think of my classic loophole? Feeling pretty silly now that you didn't think of it yourself, aren't you?" Mags looked cheerful now, with a huge bliss-ridden grin.

"Speak English, Mags. Not lawyer."

"Listen and learn, Walter. The *Citizenship and Immigration Act* says very clearly that anybody born after 1949 outside the terrestrial governance of Canada is not automatically entitled to receive Canadian citizenship, *unless he or she was born on a Canadian military ship.*"

I processed this. "So what you're saying is, anyone born on a Canadian military ship automatically gets Canadian citizenship."

"Exactly."

"And a Canadian military ship can potentially be virtually any ship, so long as someone active in the Canadian military is physically on it at the time? Is that what you're saying?"

"Yup. The ship has to be owned by a citizen of the Commonwealth, but that's about it."

"Nice."

He touched his beer can to mine again. "I told you, it's a loophole the size of your head. If a kid is born on a Canadian military ship, he or she basically gets Canadian citizenship for free."

"What about the parents?"

Mags shrugged. "They can then apply on a family class

visa. Simple. If I had the money I would buy a ship myself and fill it to the brim with pregnant-and-about-to-pop Somali pirate wives, just to piss off the feds." He hung his head. "No, I wouldn't. Actually I should probably report the finding to the Ministry of Justice so someone can recommend an amendment to the statute, not that any of those clowns listen to anyone unless you serve them with papers." Then he brightened again. "But it's cute, isn't it?"

"Impressive," I said, but I was itching to check my e-mail for absolutely no reason. And I was thinking of Marycarmen.

"Do you want to see the kid? The new one, I mean. Annie. She's sleeping but she'll wake up and start bawling any second now. You develop a sixth sense, I swear."

We probably spent five minutes in the tiny powder-pink bedroom just watching baby Annie, whose little mouth was breathing hard and inert to everything but the promise of new milk.

Kind, clever Mags with the cherubic child and the wife in a picture frame on a linoleum table, you must have read all about me by now in the hoary broadsheets that flap around our city crapping out lies and half-truths upon us all. "A little learning is a dangerous thing," said Octavian to me once, quoting Alexander Pope. That little learning you gave me – it ruined my life.

♋

The next day Octavian sauntered in at eleven.

"Call Mr. Benitez," I said, without looking up from the website I was skimming: *The Pickup Artist Bible: How To Get Any Woman To Love You Instantly. Make Them Chase You Down and Beg for Attention.* "Tell him to check his e-mail; I've sent him step-by-step instructions on what he needs to do and I've slotted him in for a conference call with his niece on Wednesday. I've also sent him an invoice."

"I should just give Mags your job. It would eliminate the

middleman. Next time you hit him up for advice, ask him if he wants me to fire you."

"Sure, Octavian. I'll tell him that. By the way, buddy, I stole your girlfriend."

Octavian's head snapped at a right angle and for a few seconds his eyes glittered, and I thought perilously about the Sig Sauer pistol. "Are we talking about little Marycarmen?"

"That's right, buddy," I said bravely, but Octavian's face had relaxed.

"You can have Marycarmen with my blessing, chum. Or should I say chump? Want me to walk her down the aisle for you?"

"Funny, she asked me the exact same thing."

"And we're all winners." He threw himself onto the sofa still in his coat and scarf, grabbed one of his Russian novels from the shelf and began to read, but I could tell he was annoyed and this pleased me immensely. Octavian the unflappable had been most artfully flapped.

"Also, have you read the *Citizenship and Immigration Act* recently? I bet you haven't. There's a loophole in it the size of your head. If you go to divisional court for me today, I'll even tell you what it is."

Octavian's gaze withered in my direction.

"I don't remember all of the details exactly. The gist of it is that anyone born on a boat with a Canadian on it is automatically a Canadian citizen. Something like that."

Octavian pounced. "Inaccurate as always, mini-brain. That's literally impossible, or every two-bit cruise ship from Bangladesh would be doing a bumper business in maternity cabins. Do you know how big the immigration business is in this city? There are literally a million lawyers in this city combing over the books for loopholes."

There was a pounding on the stairs and a chinook of lilac perfume. Marycarmen had chosen an absolutely exquisite moment to appear. She beamed beautifully and shook her hat and swishy black hair free of snow, filling the room with another current of lilac, then sashayed over to my desk and ostentatiously planted a kiss on my forehead.

"Hi honey," she said. "Miss me?" She turned around and smirked at Octavian.

"I've been thinking about you all day" escaped from my throat before I could catch myself, and I looked guiltily at Octavian, whose expression had changed to one of studied boredom.

"We're just in the middle of something, Marycarmen," I said. "Do you mind finishing up the demand letter from last week? Then we can talk."

"Don't mind me," she said, settling at the receptionist's desk, and withdrawing her phone from her purse she began to play *Penguin Race*.

"Nobody minds him," said Octavian. "He's always wrong. He was wrong as recently as one minute ago."

"Maybe," I said smugly. "But Mags is never wrong. He reads the *Annual Practice* like it's a comic book. He explained the whole scheme to me. If you don't believe me, check the *Canadian Naval War Act* for yourself. Something about how anyone born on a Canadian military ship is automatically eligible for citizenship."

"You tell him, honey," advised Marycarmen.

Octavian sprang up from the sofa. "Alright Walter," he said, in Marycarmen's general direction. "Let's see who's right."

"Mags is always right."

"Mags is a genius. You are a ruminant. You chewed up whatever it was he told you and converted it into methane."

Marycarmen laughed at that, but when Octavian grinned at her she covered her mouth and sniffed daintily. I tried to catch her eye so I could blow her a proprietary boyfriend's kiss but she was suddenly transfixed by her phone screen. Quick. Blow her away with the classic wit of Jolly Roger. Give her funnybone a good Roger-ing. My mind remained obstinate. I repaired to the Internet and searched for "Good comebacks to cow insult." None materialized, so I tried "Comeback for methane wisecrack" and then "Top one hundred all-purpose cow comebacks."

"Octavian?"

"Huh?"

"It's been twenty minutes."

"So what?"

"Well, did you find the loophole?"

"This is not possible."

I looked triumphantly at Marycarmen, who rewarded me with a flash of her little teeth.

"I told you I was right."

"It is physically impossible that even the massive cock-up that is the government of Canada could have overlooked this. This isn't a loophole, it's a black hole. Mags should be committed to an asylum. Who the hell reads the *Canadian Naval War Act* for fun? If he's right, and I think he is, then anyone with a boat has the power to create a new citizen. Do you know how desperate people are to get into this country?"

"Who's a cow now, Octavian? Moo. Want me to milk you?"

Octavian looked at me pityingly. "I suggest you reconsider that last one. Poor, poor Walter and his common, petty little ego trip. Of course you don't know how big this is. You were born here and you don't have a clue what some people would give for that. Do you know how much money is at stake here? We're literally sitting on a gold mine."

"You literally don't know what the word 'literally' means, do you Octavian?" I said.

"Come on, honey. Be nice," said Marycarmen reproachfully, reducing me to contrition with a single scarlet pout. She held up her phone and smiled: high score. I gave her the thumbs up and mouthed *Congratulations*.

"Listen to the woman, Walter," said Octavian, and Marycarmen instantly glowed with pleasure, deflating me again. "Madam secretary, could you please get Mr. Ferdinand Magellan from Parkdale Legal Aid on the phone? Then book me a room at the Cabos Melia Resort in Cuba for one week from now and send Mr. Martinez in Miami the biggest bottle of Crown Royal you can find. I need to borrow his boat." To me he said, "Walter. Cancel everything. Forget about getting run over by a bus. We need to see Mags right away."

"I don't know what you're talking about, Octavian, but if you're going to Cuba, so am I. I'm sick of being in the office six days a week, I'm sick of winter and I haven't had a vacation since before law school. I deserve a break. And what's this about being run over by a bus?"

"What you *deserve* is a beating. You work six days a week because you're incompetent, not because we're swimming in files. You spend half your time undoing your own mistakes. A competent lawyer could do what you do in forty-five minutes a day."

"And what exactly would you know about being a competent lawyer?"

"Personal injury law was supposed to be our next gig. I had a brain-wave last night. But that was yesterday. Personal injury is out. Get run over by a bus in your spare time. Today we're an immigration law firm."

ꝗꝗ

"That's the stupidest idea I've ever heard in my life," said Mags flatly. "I'm surprised at you, Octavian." We were sitting in his dismal apartment on Bathurst, eating the remains of a large Sicilian pizza at the kitchen table. The grimy window over the table was an apocalyptic vision of asphalt. A blue-eyed baby miniature of Mags sat toothless in his lap, leaking onto the pizza until Mags poked a milk bottle into its face.

"It was your idea," said Octavian.

"Maybe. But then you and Walter took a piss all over it, and I don't want it anymore," said Mags irritably. "I never told Walter to start a scam immigration business. I never told Walter to con desperate people in crappy countries into whelping out babies on a boat. First, it's so unethical it's almost beyond belief. Second, I was speaking theoretically. Third, I was sloshed. It's not a real loophole. It's an academic one. There is no way in a million years you could ever actually carry this out. Just trust me on this one. Walter is opening his mouth. He's about to ask me 'But why, Daddy? Why?' like my three-year-old. There are so many reasons that I don't even want to start listing them. It would upset my little Annie Ban-annie here to know that Daddy has such dumb friends."

Octavian snorted. The baby, transfixed, copied him exactly, spraying cookie juice onto both herself and Octavian's chin. Mags silently wiped them both.

"That's a piece of classic government-lawyer reasoning right there," said Octavian after he'd been cleaned. "If it's not allowed, it must be prohibited. In fact, it must be prohibited at all costs. Give me one reason why it won't work. The loophole is beautiful, Mags. It's foolproof. They should appoint you to the Supreme Court for this."

"That's the first smart thing you've said all day. Fine, Octavian. Let's start with the most obvious thing. Where are you two seafaring seamen planning to procure a boat? And by 'seamen', I do mean the seminal fluid, by the way."

"Easy-peasy," I said. "Tell him, Octavian."

"My cousin sails to Miami twice a year in a fifteen-foot yacht," said Octavian. "He has a man named Martinez who smuggles cigars for him out of the Marina Hemingway outside of Havana and he's given me *carte blanche* to borrow his boat. And Mags, we already have a client lined up. During my last trip to Varadero I met a guy named Ramón at a Ministry of Tourism function. I've never met anyone so eager to get off that island. Ramón promised me his life savings and some sexual favours I didn't even know existed if I could smuggle him back to Canada."

"I know Walter reads at a fourth-grade level," said Mags, "but you should be ashamed, Octavian. Have you ever heard of a little thing called the Bay of Pigs? There's an American embargo on Cuba. The traffic between Miami and Havana is in one direction only, and not all of it survives."

I clapped Mags on the back. "Thanks for the compliment, buddy. Really. You boys are the best friends a guy could ask for."

"I have a Canadian boat and a means of conveyance, just as the loophole requires," said Octavian.

"Did you hear that?" said Mags, bouncing baby Annie on his knee. "The brown man says he has a system to beat the U.S. Coast Guard. Daddy associates with criminals now."

"Baa," said Annie.

"Point taken, Mags," I argued. "But let's just say that Octavian can get the boat into Cuba. That would be pretty sweet, wouldn't it?"

"No. It would be stupid. Even if by some miracle you could sail from Miami to Cuba without being arrested, or preferably shot, even if you do manage to con some poor Cuban woman into believing that giving birth on your rust bucket will infuse her baby with magical Canadian superpowers, do you really think the feds are going to sit back and clap while you two dummies make a mockery of the system? They'll destroy you. What's Plan B, may I ask? Will you bribe them? Bump them off?"

"Of course not," said Octavian, deeply offended. "Murder is illegal."

"They'll have no choice but to co-operate," I argued. "It's the law. You've proved that it's the law. Isn't it the law?"

"Are you retarded, Walter? Do you honestly believe that when babies are born, little passports fall on them from heaven, just because it's the law? No. Bureaucrats have to issue them and believe me they won't like it. Law or no law, they'll screw your clients, if you can get any, as hard as they possibly can."

"Have faith," said Octavian airily. "I'm a superstar at the game of bureaucracy. How do you think I managed to get my own citizenship so fast? I have all the time in the world for this and I'm exceedingly patient. Mags, tell me something. Have you ever been to Cuba?"

"Do you have any idea how many kids I have? Do I look like I can afford to go to Cuba? I haven't had a vacation in years," snapped Mags.

"Well, then let me tell you something," said Octavian. "Just last fall three Cuban ballet dancers doing a production of *Swan*

Lake in Toronto refused to board the plane back to Cuba. The week before that, a Cuban soccer player defected during a friendly in Montréal. The guy had a wife and a mother and a brother, but he left them all behind with nothing but the clothes on his back, and all for what? For the chance to wash dishes in a scummy diner in Montréal. Why? You tell me. Cuba is a communist dictatorship. You make fifteen dollars a month and live in a house with your mother and two uncles and six cousins eating rice and beans fourteen times a week. You study for six years to be a civil engineer and then you call in every favour you have just to get a lousy-paying job mopping up tourist puke in the resort cafeteria."

"Check this out," I said, thumbing my omniscient cell phone. "Fidel Castro in 1992 said: 'There are hookers, but prostitution is not allowed in our country. There are no women forced to sell themselves to a man, to a foreigner, to a tourist. Those who do so do it on their own, voluntarily.... We can say that they are highly educated hookers and quite healthy, because we are the country with the lowest number of AIDS cases'. Castro, Octavian, any relation?"

"Second," continued Octavian without missing a beat, "who says we have to stay in Cuba? If everything works out with my cousin's boat we'll buy our own boat and move on to bigger game. India. Mexico. China. They're all pumping out people by the millions. Bogotá is one giant smokestack. It's so crowded in Mexico City that you can barely move. Canada's population density is about three people per square kilometre. Don't you think that's a little bit selfish?"

Mags clasped the baby's fat little hands in his own and clapped them, making Annie squeal with delight. "And the best part is," he said sarcastically, "it's all for charity."

"That's not even a joke," said Octavian. "Thousands of people all over the world would give years of their lives and most of their money to immigrate to this country. We're not recruiting Colombian drug lords, Mags. We'll be giving good hard-working people a fair shot at the immigration system. And the beauty is, it's all legal."

"Mags," I said. "The way I see it is, all of us are failing at life right now –"

"Easy there, Señor Mouth," said Octavian.

"I don't know or want to know where you get your pocket money from, Octavian. Me and Mags here don't have rich daddies. Listen Mags, the Castro and Roger Professional Legal Corporation is bleeding cash. At this rate my main motivation for living is that I'll probably die before I pay off my student loans. I still live with my mother. And you. Do you want to be a part-time naval reservist for the rest of your life? Do you want to raise your kids in this slum? No offence. This is about helping people. And if we charge a fair price in the process, so what? That's what capitalism is all about."

"Ba!" announced Annie, drooling. "Ba ba ba."

"Shhh, nap time soon," soothed Mags. He pulled Annie from his lap and held her wiggling and giggling up to his face.

"Well?" said Octavian.

"Well what?"

"Well, are you in?"

"What do you mean, am I in? Am I in what? A mental asylum? What does it have to do with me? You want to go to Cuba and play doctor at sea, be my guest. You want to get yourself disbarred for immoral conduct, knock yourself out. Daddy here finally gets a week of vacation in a couple of days and he intends to enjoy it."

"We need you on board with us, Mags," said Octavian. "Literally and figuratively. You're the missing piece of the puzzle. The loophole isn't complete without you. It's not a Canadian military vessel unless an active member of the Canadian armed forces is physically present on it."

Mags shook his head violently. "Don't even start. I'm not even really in the military, I'm just in the –"

"The Naval Reserve," finished Octavian. "Which absolutely counts. If you're in the Naval Reserve, you're a bona fide member of the official Armed Forces. Your presence on our boat will make it an official Canadian military ship. We can't do this without you, Mags. Need I even insult you by saying that we'll split everything fifty-fifty?"

"You mean thirty-thirty-thirty," I said. "No, I mean thirty-three –"

"You can have some too," said Octavian briefly.

"No," said Mags.

"Please?" I said.

"Hell no."

"It's foolproof."

"No it's not. It's unethical and preposterous."

"But entirely legal," said Octavian. "The greatest loophole of all time."

Mags dropped his affronted, intent stare and looked down at baby Annie, who gazed back up at him dopey-eyed and yawning.

"I can offer a bribe," said Octavian. "Where are you going for your vacation?"

"It's not a vacation, alright? It's a staycation."

"A staycation. Oh, that's fantastic. And what have you got lined up for this staycation of yours? Snow shovelling? Pneumonia? How about an all-expenses-paid vacation to a Cuban resort for you and your family? I'm from a big family Mags, I know what it's like. Wait until you see the wonders a little rest and relaxation will work on your wife. She'll be pregnant again by the end of the trip, I personally guarantee it, even if I have to do it myself. I'll need your services for one night only. Do whatever you want for the rest of the time. Cuba is heaven on earth. In Varadero you'd be in shorts and shades taking baby here for ice cream."

Mags looked at him and muttered, "Babies don't eat ice cream."

"You can eat hers, then," said Octavian, looking at Annie with a credible expression of tenderness. "What a beauty! She wants to come to Uncle, doesn't she? Hand her over, Mags."

Uncertainly Mags handed over his baby to Octavian, who softly rubbed her back until her eyelids began to droop.

"One night," said Mags. "And all I'd have to do is sit there. You'll provide the boat and the clients. If you're missing one or both, it's not my problem. I'm just on vacation."

"Precisely, Mags. You just take an all-expenses-paid vacation and enjoy. We'll do all the solicitor work. Say yes and I'll call the client right now."

Mags was silent for a minute.

"I want to talk to my wife," he said finally.

"Is that a yes?" I said.

"No!" barked Mags. "Now go away. Maxine will be back any minute. I wish."

"Take it easy, Mags," said Octavian.

We walked back to Octavian's sleek sedan in the chill wind on Bathurst. There was snow all over the windshield, but it was dry snow and Octavian brushed it away easily with his glove.

"Do you think he'll say yes?" I asked.

Octavian put the key in the ignition. "He should have bargained," he said.

ԶԶ

I was feeling good when Octavian dropped me back at the office. I felt so good that I didn't even whinge when he mumbled something about a date with Yamaira and tore off into the dim winter sunset, leaving me to inhale the offerings of his exhaust pipe mingled with the fumes of the Zaika restaurant's korma special. Inside, Marycarmen was perched at the reception desk, thumbing at her phone.

"I'm feeling great, baby," I said, flinging my coat onto the sofa like a prizefighter and leaning over the desk to nuzzle her hair with my nose. "Miss me much?"

"You are so sweet, Walter. Is Octavian coming too?"

"No, he has a date. I had a great day. One of the best days I've had in a while. In a few weeks I'll be rolling in cash and some of it may even land on you, baby girl."

She leaned over violet-scented and kissed me, making my head spin. "What, he has a new girlfriend already?"

"Why do you care, Marycarmen? You're my girlfriend now, right? I'm trying to tell you something important. All of those jerks who spat me out in law school will regret the day they crossed Walter Roger. You, my little burrito, are looking at one of only three people on planet Earth privy to a serious loophole in a federal statute."

"Of course I'm your girlfriend, Walter." Then she frowned. "Is this the immigration thing you guys were talking about yesterday? With the boat? How if you read the *Naval War Act* basically anyone can be a Canadian citizen if they're born on a ship with an army guy on it?"

"I thought you were playing *Penguin Race* yesterday."

"I can multi-task."

"Anyway, Marycarmen, tonight we had our big strategy meeting to review some of the fine print. Complex legal questions and such. We've got one of the top lawyers in town on board, not to mention yours truly. We're going to turn this place around, I tell you. I feel like a new man."

"I don't think it will work, Walter."

I drew back from her floral cloud. "What are you talking about, girl? Why not?"

"The *Citizenship Act* requires an external witness to the birth, usually a medical professional like a nurse. I don't know how it works in offshore jurisdictions, but did you ever consider that maybe, just maybe, expectant mothers might not want to deliver their babies with no one around but lawyers?"

"Did you just say 'jurisdiction'?"

She smirked prettily. "I listen when you and Octavian are talking. There's nothing else to do around here anyway."

"There's plenty to do around here. Just nobody does it except me!"

"Everyone else at the firm is going to Cuba. Come on Walter, we'll have so much fun."

"The firm has exactly two people in it – baby, why are we even having this argument? Of course you can come to Cuba. In fact, let's go and celebrate right now. Margaritas on me."

She beamed and leaned towards me exactly as the office phone rang. "Could you answer that please?"

"I would love to *mi amor*, but I have to study. I've got an exam tomorrow." She slithered out of my arms and swept out

with all of her fragrant plumage.

With our secretary under the impression that all work was strictly voluntary and my partner strangely preoccupied with online music videos, I knew that I would pay dearly for my absence in the screams of angry clients, but I was feeling too good to care. In a few short days I would be airborne, and with any luck we would be minting new Canadian citizens for cash on a luxury boat in Cuba before the week was out. It occurred to me that I hadn't thought about driving a Maserati XL 500, bought and paid for with my staggering senior partner's bonus, in a very long time. These days I disposed of time by thinking of Marycarmen in a string bikini, and now I could practically feel her in a steaming hotel room in Havana: mine, mine, mine.

Part 2:

Tempt Not a Desperate Man
Havana

Chapter 6
Havana

When I look back at the whole sordid episode, there was really no reason for me to accompany Octavian to Cuba. He had clout and contacts all over South America; I only had an urgent hunger to escape my life, cramped in a little desk over the Indo-Pak restaurant, and the conviction that as the grand architect of our money-spinning plot I was entitled to a little reward. *Treat yourself, because you're worth it,* cajoled a voice in my head. Whether the voice was an excess of self-esteem induced by my sudden transformation into a boyfriend, or an amalgam of too many shampoo commercials, I had convinced myself that a week in Cuba was imperative to my health and well-being. Give me Havana, or give me death. The problem was that, just like everything else in my life, I couldn't really afford it. I'd asked my mother to loan me the money for a museum-walking tour of Washington, D.C. with Octavian that was really a seven-day boozing spree in the Caribbean.

"But honey," she'd said, puzzled. "Why would you need a loan to go on vacation? You're a successful lawyer. Aren't you?"

Of course I was. I'd forgotten that lawyers are all million-aires. Never mind. Ever since I'd started making regular payments on my student loan, my credit limit had increased, so I drew a little more, springing for a ticket for Marycarmen as well, burrowing deeper into debt like a racoon in a rubbish tip. I didn't care. With the new turn our business was taking, I'd calculated, I would pay it back in a month or two.

When the plane landed in Varadero it was pitch-black outside and so hot that steam rose from the cracks in the airport runway. The airport itself was small, but its fixtures gleamed bright and modern and the deeply tanned Cubans who manned it all spoke courteous and only slightly accented English. A border guard in a military-style uniform at passport control issued me a detachable thirty-day tourist visa that could be crumpled and discarded upon exit – a neat device that enabled Canadians who subsequently visited the U.S. to pretend that they'd never so much as dreamed of visiting a forbidden communist paradise. The guard was also kind enough to direct me to the *Cadeca* office in the Departures Hall, where I gleefully anticipated becoming a peso millionaire.

"What is it, ten thousand pesos to a dollar?" I said to the woman at the *Cadeca*.

"No peso," she said. "Only C.U.C. Convertible peso."

She exchanged my green twenty-dollar bills for an almost equivalent number of *veinte peso* papers. It was my first introduction to the world's fakest currency. In Cuba tourists are forbidden from using the worthless local peso and are instead forced to buy everything in C.U.C. at hugely inflated prices.

Outside the airport I found a cross-looking cab driver with a sweating head who refused to quote me a price, only glared at me in the darkness in the rear-view mirror and turned up the volume on the radio every time I attempted to speak. To spite him with white noise, I rolled down the car windows and the warm wind on my face was wonderful. After about twenty minutes of cruising I could smell the salt from the ocean. If it hadn't been nearly midnight I might have asked Road Rage to pull me over for a quick dip.

When we pulled into the wide circular driveway of what was apparently our hotel, I was certain that Marycarmen had made yet another one of her lavish mistakes. I'd assumed we would stay at the most pitiful hotel that communist pesos could buy. The Cabos Melia was clearly a luxury resort, with lamp-lit stucco archways over a spacious patio and pots of pink roses garlanding the swirling stairs of a marble swimming pool. In the dim light I couldn't see much of the grounds, but I could hear the rustle of palm trees and the crash of waves on a nearby beach. The cab driver emitted a simian grunt to communicate that I should hurry up and pay my fare, which I did as disdainfully as I could before he tore away.

"He was cheating you," came the bored voice of Octavian from somewhere in the middle of the swimming pool. His head surfaced in the blueness and he looked at me gravely like a watery Don Corleone. "The cab driver. He was covering the meter with his elbow. Even Mags could see it, and he's legally blind without his glasses."

I turned around to see Mags beaming at me on the patio with his bad teeth in a short purple caftan. His skin glowed a healthy pink and he had a Cristal beer tucked under each arm.

"*Hola amigo*," he said. "Welcome to the Cabos Melia all-inclusive resort, also known as heaven. Octavian was right. What a fabulous place. I left the kids with the on-site babysitters and tried windsurfing. I haven't felt this fit since basic training. Maxine slept all day under a beach umbrella and they even have a kosher buffet. I ate an entire pan of brisket with spicy ketchup. I mean the whole thing."

"Be a buddy and give me one of those beers."

"I didn't even tell you about the best part of my day, Walter," said Mags. "After dinner Maxine and I went back to our room and for the second time in two nights we actually —"

"Stop right there, Mags."

"Don't be a blue-collar prude, Walter," said Octavian. "I'm glad you're enjoying yourself, Mags, because in a couple of days we'll be calling you in for active duty. You've astutely observed that this resort is far too good for both of you —"

"Wrong. It's perfect," said Mags, standing with his legs apart so the ocean breeze rippled his short caftan dangerously high.

"But our client insisted we stay here. Ramón has some serious clout at the Ministry of Tourism. His wife works here at the concierge desk and they're both hot for our deal. Actually, they couldn't care less about our deal, they just want to bust out of Cuba. When I showed them my Canadian passport I thought Ramón would flat-out steal it. Maybe he's killed someone," he added.

Mags shook the last drops of beer onto his tongue and signalled to the bartender. "Very nice, Octavian. That's some high-quality clientele you've managed to recruit for your dumb project."

"*Our* dumb project."

"Don't tell me you've actually managed to trick some poor pregnant lady into giving birth on your toy boat."

"I certainly have," said Octavian. "In fact, Ramón wants to drive us to Havana for a tour of the city. That should give us some time to talk."

"I'm not coming," said Mags. "Because (a), me actually doing anything besides sitting on a boat wasn't part of the deal, and (b) Maxine and me have couples massage booked for after breakfast with Señora Ursula. She uses aromatherapy. It's part of the package."

"I have plans too, Octavian," I piped up. "I want to go scuba diving and then I want to go to the buffet and load up on red meat. Marycarmen gets here tomorrow night and I need my energy, if you know what I mean."

"Fortunately for you spoiled first-world brats, Ramón is busy all day today. We'll meet them tomorrow after Estella's shift. And could you please keep your voices down? Listen to yourselves. Loved that delicious buffet today, did you, Mags? The chunk of cow you ate today in one lunch sitting is probably more meat than the average Cuban gets in two weeks."

"Tell them to meet us for dinner tonight," I said. "I hear these resorts have amazing restaurants. Maybe they can spot us their employee discount. Oh wait, I forgot, it's all free."

"Oh heavens, yes," said Mags, his bug eyes popping. "Last night Maxine and I had dinner by candlelight. She had the blue crab bisque and salmon mousse. I had the red snapper stuffed with olive and eggplant. After dinner when the kids fell asleep I can truthfully tell you that it was the first time since the last kid was born that we actually –"

"Alright Mags," I said. I drained another can of beer. "We get it. You are sexually active. Congratulations. Now focus."

Octavian shook his head. "No candlelight dinners. We can't do anything too conspicuous, and the workers aren't allowed to use any of the resort facilities anyway. As for your quaint notion of an employee discount in a communist dictatorship, Walter, the less said about it the better."

"*A bientôt* then," said Mags, sweeping away. "My wife awaits me."

"Lawyer-client privilege, Mags. You should apply it to your marital life occasionally," called Octavian, but Mags had broken into a sprint, his caftan billowing behind him. "By the way, Walter. This is a couples resort, so we're sharing a room. I hope your homosexual prejudices aren't affronted. Nonetheless I would ask you to avoid either touching or looking at me once we get there. Better still, make it a general rule for all of our present and future interactions."

The patio as we walked out into the lobby smelled of musk roses. Our second floor room was filled with breezes, the bed linen was crisp and fragrant, the complimentary shampoo was zesty and viscous, and Octavian snored all night like a truck driver with emphysema.

 QQ

When I was very young my mother read me an English children's story about a magical land called Take-What-You-Want. The hero of the story, whom I distinctly recall had a vaguely rude anatomical name like Fannie or Dick or Sausage Botty, spent a blissful day taking whatever he wanted from the shops of Take-What-You-Want without payment or consequence. At some point his orgiastic acquisition of free puppies and liquorice allsorts engendered some terrible outcome and our hero learned a wholesome life lesson about the value of self-denial.

The Cabos Melia Resort in Cuba was the land of Take-What-You-Want with an important difference: the only lesson I learned about self-denial was that it was unpleasant. Nearly any whim I had was instantly gratified, and it was fantastic. When I was hungry I waddled over to the seaside grill and the chef barbecued me a fish and served it to me with a flourish. When I was too hot to sunbathe, but too lazy for the brisk walk to the ocean, I went swimming in the pretty blue water of the enormous palm-tree shaped hotel pool. And if I swam a little too far or a little too fast and suddenly found myself thirsty, a bartender in a little bathing suit at the handsome beach bar would swiftly make me a tall ice-cold Long Island Iced Tea.

At lunchtime I sauntered over to the sumptuous dining room on the main floor, which was filled with Germans methodically depositing slices of meat into their pink mouths. I followed suit and made myself a platter of sliced mammals and decorated it with several rocks of exotic cheese. I heaped a second plate with tarts and slivers of various fruit pies, but when it came to actually eating them I was stuffed and could manage only one bite of each before discarding the rest. What was that look on the young waiter's face as he wordlessly cleared away my half-eaten plate, and what did it matter? I dashed away as soon as I'd finished eating and plunged like a pot-bellied penguin into the ocean.

The beach was full of Germans. They were easy to spot because they were solidly built, deathly serious and mostly nude. They all woke up at the crack of dawn to nab the best towels and could be seen carefully calibrating their beach chairs to the precise angle of the sun's rays to ensure optimal sunbathing. They all read books. They all probably read the same book. I was afraid of the Germans.

Sometime in the middle of the morning I fancied a beer, and it occurred to me that I could have one. It occurred to me that I could have ten if it pleased me, and not one of the Cubans paid to attend me as I lounged in the sunshine on my beach chair would have a single thing to say about it. I was on my sixth Cristal beer when I spotted Octavian in rolled-up trousers, galloping barefoot toward me in the surf with the sun shining behind him. The water, which was precisely turquoise, shimmered like molten glass.

"Hey buddy," I said, slinging my drink at him, "Want some?"

"You've had more than enough, Walter. Get up and get moving. Change of plan. We're meeting our clients now. Estella just started her shift."

"Shouldn't I change first?"

He tugged me upright and began dragging me to the main complex. "No, for once your outfit is perfect. Boozy red face. Disgusting baseball cap. You look exactly like a tourist. For some reason Ramón got jumpy as hell. Just be discreet."

"Prepare for my communist grenade launch," I bellowed, throwing sand in Octavian's face. "Beware the Bay of Pigs."

"That's actually not bad," he said, grimacing. "Idiots are non-threatening, and no one would say something so stupid unless he was genuinely an idiot."

We walked past the sunbathers toasting their bloated post-buffet breakfast flesh, past the long rows of sun chairs and the beachfront bar and grill until we reached the Spanish-style lobby, which was furnished with low sofas and English magazines. Resort life at the Cabos Melia was engineered to destroy any shred of evidence that Cuba is actually a foreign country. There was no trace of the Spanish language anywhere, for instance. English was more than the *lingua franca* – it was ubiquitous. Even the maids could warble a word or two, and the concierges all seemed to be word-perfect.

Today the young woman at the concierge desk was vastly pregnant, but endeavoured to minimize it by buttoning a navy blue blazer tightly over her resort uniform of white shirt and tan trousers. Her hairstyle, dyed red and styled high in an elaborate arrangement of curls, also seemed calculated to draw attention upwards rather than outwards. She was on the telephone but her eyes were darting hither and thither and when she saw us watching her she hung up.

"Good afternoon," she said, high, clear, artificial, smiling, with the same definite but unintrusive accent of my waitress that morning. "Are you enjoying the Cabos Melia?"

"Absolutely," I said. "I'm having an incredible time."

"Two of my cousins immigrated to Toronto, and one of them is actually expecting a child next month," began Octavian, but she shook her crown of henna-red plaits almost violently and said, "Please let me know if there is anything I can do to make your stay more comfortable, sirs." She lowered her voice. "My husband is waiting for you outside. Tonight he will tell me."

"It was our pleasure to meet you, Estella," I said, and Octavian flashed one of his reassuring handsome smiles. We walked out through the big marble arches to the circular driveway, where a baby blue Peugeot stood waiting. There was a man leaning against a palm tree smoking a cigarette in a natty tan blazer despite the heat. He was young, scarcely older than I was, and completely Spanish in appearance with black hair and surprising green eyes.

"Who's he?" he said, flicking his green eyes in my direction.

"My partner," said Octavian. "A top-of-the-line lawyer. You don't get much better than this guy."

"Walter Roger," I said.

"Ramón Iguarez," said the man, quick and unsmiling as he opened the doors for us.

We both climbed into the back of the car, and only when both doors had shut and we were safely cruising down the parkway did Octavian say in his smooth trust-me-I'm-a-lawyer voice, "How are you doing, Ramón?"

"I've been enjoying your beautiful country, Ramón," I said. "What an amazing beach. The water is absolutely perfect. I've never seen anything like it in my life."

The man's intense green eyes darted at me in the rear-view mirror. "That's Cuba. This country is no good for nothing but holidays. For holiday – great. For living –" He exhaled contemptuously.

There was a silence, which Octavian punctuated by shooting me a death stare, so I looked away from the mirror and watched the scenery, the tall sloping palm trees and plains of hazy grass as we drove into the vast hilly spaces surrounding the Cabos Melia.

"You guys are Canadians," announced Ramón Iguarez, driving with one hand, leaving the other free to gesticulate. "I like Canadian people. They are –" He paused. "Normal." He grinned suddenly like a flash of lightning in the rear-view mirror and gave us the thumbs-up. "That's what we say up at the Ministry. We like Canadian peoples to visit. Not like

Italians. Italians are crazy guys. They taxi into the city and yell at people. Women, men, it don't matter. They want to stop every minute. I want beer! Get me a beer! Russians are some crazy guys too."

"I saw some Russians this morning. They were having vodka and orange juice. For breakfast," I said.

"Breakfast!" scoffed Ramón. "Not only breakfast. I'm telling you twenty-four hours vodka. Vodka for breakfast, vodka for lunch, rum for dessert. More crazy guys. You know who else? Germans. I'm telling you. They sit on the beaches like this –" he pulled a long face of small-eyed solemnity in the rear-view mirror – "and they never say nothing except 'Mister, could you please turn down the volume?' Yeah, I like Canadians. Canadian people are normal."

"We try," I said modestly. "By the way, should I wear a seat belt? I mean, is it mandatory in Cuba?"

"What difference does it make?" said Ramón.

"Tell me, Ramón. Where are we going today?" said Octavian.

The man shrugged. "To La Habana. I'll drive you to the Cathedral San Cristobal, take a walk on the Malecón, you can look at the old American cars downtown. What, you want to see the Capitol too? Sure. Always the same things. Always the same questions."

We sat there in silence for a moment.

"Sounds great," I said. "I've heard great things about the Capitol."

He eyed me moodily in the rear-view mirror. "We had the International Tourism Fair here in Habana last year. You know what everybody is asking me? How much money people make. You want to know how much money my wife makes at the hotel? You there, the drunk."

"I would imagine not much," said Octavian. "I would imagine maybe thirty C.U.C. a month."

Ramón looked approvingly at Octavian. "You would imagine right, my friend." Then he turned the radio up loud and began mouthing along to a garish Spanish pop song, eyeing us in the rear-view mirror as we zipped past some bare-chested men trimming tall grasses on the roadside with scythes. Octavian looked straight ahead.

"That's not a lot of money," I said.

"Oh yeah?" flared Ramón. "And how about you? Have you got lots of money? I got two cars, mister. And you know how I got them in this country? By using my brains."

"I didn't mean to be offensive –"

"Canadian peoples," said Ramón, flipping the radio off again. "Canadian peoples – they have it pretty good. I know that. I got a lot of friends all over the world from doing this job. I got – how do you say it? I'm sorry. Sometimes my English is –"

"Oh, don't worry at all. Your English is just fine, it's –"

"My English is still better than your Spanish, hey, sir?" said Ramón, hostile. "I got friends. I got *connected*. Canada is a good country. Mr. Martinez told me about you." He looked at Octavian. "You are another crazy guy."

"Mr. Martinez and me are old friends," said Octavian in his most affable lawyer tone, but he threw me a sidelong hesitant glance. "I helped him with his own immigration papers. As you probably know."

Ramón seemed to want to avoid veering the conversation in that direction. "You know what else they ask me?" he said, nearly cutting off a dilapidated truck to face me. "You know what everybody wants to know? How much does everything cost?"

"Fine," I said. "How much does everything cost? Hey, we're going pretty fast."

Ramón ignored me and continued to burn down the highway. "Do you know what my wife's sister has to do to get a little extra meat? Do you understand? Black, black, black, black market. Too black. Everything black. And they all want something from me. Everybody with their hand in my pocket. I got to get out. I got to get out of here before I get even crazier."

"You take care of them," soothed Octavian.

"It's damn well time somebody took care of me. Always I gotta take care of myself."

"Why don't we talk about the —" began Octavian, but Ramón thrust his chin out at me again.

"You like rice and beans?"

"Love them," I said, hoping that we could agree on that at the very least. "My mother makes amazing baked beans."

"Oh, you love them, do you? Let's see how much you like it when you never get nothing else." He rolled the Peugeot to a halt. A truck with its paint peeling had somehow jammed itself into a sinkhole ahead of us on the roadside and a troop of small, deeply tanned men were trying to wrestle it out. Wordlessly Ramón parked the car and jumped out to help them. We were roasting hot but somehow we felt too conspicuous to participate; even Octavian, for all his dark hair and olive skin, was too tall and too cleanly shaven, too finicky in his crisp shirt for that company of sturdy brown Cubans.

"Do you know those guys?" I asked, when Ramón returned.

He fired up the engine. "No."

"What happened?"

"Nothing."

In the window Cuba whizzed past me at one hundred and forty kilometres an hour, the occasional half-crumbled building sinking into the swamp. In one of the hills an arrangement of huge white block letters read "LA HABANA."

"How long have you been with the Ministry of Tourism, Ramón?" asked Octavian.

"A while," said Ramón. "Why? You don't think I'm a welcoming guy? I'm a very friendly guy. I got friends all over the place."

"Not at all, but you know and I know that most young guys at the Ministry of Tourism can't afford two cars. You must be a pretty smart guy."

Ramón looked pleased by this. "I want to make money. Do you want to make money?"

"Everyone wants to make money."

"Exactly," said Ramón. "I'm a mechanical engineer. For six years I stayed at my desk and I ate books for breakfast. I drank books for lunch. Every night I stayed up until three in the morning reading my books. Why? What did I do it for?" He snorted and turned up the volume on the radio, then turned it down again. "You saw my wife. For five years she studied economics. Did she get a job? No. Then we went to tourism school for two years. Why two years?" he said, and tapped his head a few times. "They know how tourists talk. They got to make sure you don't get no ideas. And English. You got to know English good, even if you want to be a cleaner. A lot of these really young guys, they want to be singers and dancers. Those boys make good money."

"I actually talked to one of the guitar players last night," I said. "He was really good. Seemed like a nice guy too. Julio."

"I put Julio there," said Ramón sharply. "I hope you tipped well."

"I see," said Octavian.

"Here in Cuba we're just a bunch of nice guys. No police, no Fidel, no nothing. No offense meant, Octavian."

"None taken. I've never even met the man."

"But you're still family. You have influence."

"Could be."

"The music was amazing. The guy had talent, he was playing Beethoven right on the beach," I said nervously. We were in the city limits but Ramón was still weaving at top speed.

"You like him so much," said Ramón, drawing a cigarette from his breast pocket and lighting it one-handed, "you stay here and live with him. Me, I'm gonna do whatever I can to get me and my family off this island."

Ramón puffed away at his cigarette without speaking, and finally ground the taxi to a halt alongside a hulking limestone building with iron grilles on its windows. The cobblestone street was worn thin and everything in it, even the mangy dog that loped over to us to beg with its eyes, seemed to be covered in dust.

"Here we are," said Ramón, the cigarette still in his mouth. "It's Old Havana. I'll meet you in front of the Cathedral later. Plaza de la Catedral. You get lost, ask anyone for directions. Everyone knows it."

"I'd hoped to have a word with you, Ramón," said Octavian, as easy as ever. "Would you care to join us for lunch? If you'd prefer, we can invite our friend Mr. Martinez for the discussion as well."

"This is Old Havana, go see the Cathedral," said Ramón. "We don't have nothing to discuss. I already know everything, thanks to your friend Mr. Martinez. I even scoped out your boat at the Marina Hemingway. He told me your price, and I'm telling you it's too high."

"Our fee is firm," said Octavian.

"You lawyers, no matter where you come from you're all the same. You want to know a joke? I'll tell you a joke. A man walks into a bar with an alligator. 'Do you serve lawyers in here?' the man asks. 'Sure, we serve lawyers!' says the bartender. The man says, 'Great! I'll have a Cristal, and for my 'gator, one lawyer'. I wish I had a 'gator sometimes."

Octavian laughed. "Like you said, some things are the same no matter where you're from. Go to any country on the planet and lawyers are the devil. Do I look like the devil to you, Ramón?"

"If the devil ran a ferry to Miami I'd be the first man on it. Three years now we've put our names in for the immigration lottery to America. All of these applications, you know what they cost? Money. Do you think I have money? If the devil wanted my soul, I'd say take it. But don't take my money. You think I don't know you've never done this before? Your friend there drunk in the backseat. He's a clown."

"We know what we're doing," said Octavian.

"When will we know to find you?" I asked.

Ramón made no reply to either one of us, only turned abruptly back to the car and drove off tipping his cigarette out the front window. We had been dismissed.

ଯଯ

We drove back to Varadero in a chilly silence. Octavian and I had toured all of Old Havana, the Plaza de la Revolución,

John Lennon Park, and at Octavian's insistence, the US Special Interests Building, where a guard in full army kit waved a gun at me when I overzealously took too many pictures with my phone. Shaken, we beat a hasty retreat back to the Malecón, the sea wall that runs along the Havana coastline, and watched teenage boys perched upon it throw stones into the water. As we panted in the heat, a pair of women in faded shorts and tank tops sidled up to us with their arms linked and said things that sounded like "Hi honey" and "Hi *chulo*." One of them – the prettier one, with a big wide-eyed face and cute gappy teeth – even stroked my neck a little bit as she cooed at me in Spanish. Inordinately pleased that she had chosen me and not Octavian, I introduced myself as the CEO of Rogers' International Law and Investment Firm and offered her a drink, but Octavian seized my arm and kept marching.

"What did you do that for? That brunette was really into me," I said.

"Those girls were professionals, jerk-brain," said Octavian.

"So? They looked really nice. Maybe they just wanted to talk. Maybe they wanted to sample some white meat."

"They're *jineteras*," said Octavian. "They specialize in swindling tourists. Save your energy for your precious girlfriend."

At my insistence we took a tour of the famous Partagás cigar factory and then Octavian had an expensive drink at La Bodeguita del Medio, the hole-in-the-wall bar once favoured by Ernest Hemingway, nodding to the music like a man in ecstasy as he sipped. After a few minutes the song changed to some kind of a garish jingle with an ape's bellow as the chorus, and Octavian froze.

"What?"

"That song," he said wondrously. "It's one of mine."

"What do you mean, it's one of yours?"

He beamed at me and the bored, indolent, superior expression he habitually wore was gone. "We made the video for this song just outside of Miami. They're playing my song at Hemingway's bar. Can you believe that?"

I knew better than to bother asking who "we" were, or exactly when he had morphed into a Latin music mogul, but suddenly Octavian's preoccupation with Spanish music videos and peculiar indifference to the law firm he'd founded made a lot more sense.

"Well, good for you, Octavian," I said awkwardly. "What's the song called?"

"It's called *The Dancing Gorilla*," he said.

"Your family must be proud."

He glared at me. "They have no idea. My father thinks I run a successful law firm."

"So does my mother. Why don't you just tell them that you're a – whatever it is you are?"

"Producer."

"Fine. Tell them you're a producer."

He shrugged. "If *Gorilla* hits it big, maybe I will. If they do not respect my art, they will at least respect my money."

With time to kill, we ventured a little farther from the centre, where the big fortress-like capitol buildings yielded to apartments with peeling paint and rusty gates and sagging rotten bricks. One apartment building was actually crooked, leaning perilously away from the vertical; on the third floor where one of the walls was missing you could see someone's grandmother in a cotton housedress bent over a sink and scrubbing at some ancient pot.

We found Ramón exactly where he'd said he would be some hours later, leaning against the blue Peugeot in front of the Plaza de la Catedral. Expressionless, he opened the passenger-side doors, first one and then the other.

"Thanks," I said. Octavian said nothing, and Ramón started the engine.

"Life's a beach, hey?" he shot back and we drove in a constipated silence that I could hardly bear. Havana had sobered me, but I've never been able to withstand the sort of resentful, grudge-holding quiet that is the aftermath of a near-argument. Bianca had been the queen of silence, and my inability to decipher it had driven her to fury more than once.

"So, Ramón. There was a plaque at the Plaza de Armas that said the founder of Havana was a man named Céspedes," I said. "Do you have any idea when the city was first built?"

"Fifteen hundreds, sixteen hundreds," said Ramón indifferently. He turned the radio up to a deafening volume and this time he didn't lower it until we were rounding the oval driveway at the Cabos Melia. When he turned off the engine, I handed him a few small bills as a tip, and only realized later that I had given him the equivalent of a week's salary. He didn't thank me.

"You don't know or care when Céspedes founded Havana, do you?" said Octavian quietly. "Half of my family are engineers, you know. Engineers are all the same and you're an engineer through and through if I've ever seen one. Engineers don't care about irrelevant details. They only care about the solution. Does it matter when Havana was built? Havana exists whether you know this or not, therefore you choose not to know. Havana isn't fixable, not by engineers like you anyway. Your life is a different story. Your life might be something you can fix. That's why you're talking to me even though you think I'm crazy."

Ramón turned around sharply to face him. "For you it's just business. For me it's life. Do you know how much I would risk by trusting you, Señor Octavian? What kind of a man takes that kind of risk?"

"A smart man. A man who wants everything for his family."

Ramón's face broke into the grin he'd greeted us with that morning, the cocky grin that flashed quick and bright like lightning, and he took Octavian's hand and slowly shook it.

Octavian shook his head. "I can't close a deal with you until I know you absolutely understand the loophole."

"I graduated from the Universidad de La Habana with a degree in electrical engineering. You think that's so easy, you try it. I'm poor. I'm not stupid," said Ramón.

"And you're not poor either, if you can afford our fee."

"That's a lawyer for you. Always sticking his hands in another man's pocket."

"There are no guarantees," warned Octavian.

Ramón set his lips tightly. "When my wife's time is near we'll meet you at the Marina Hemingway and I can tell you right now I don't like to be kept waiting. If you lawyers fail, I swear to God in heaven I'm going to jump off your boat and swim to Miami with my son."

"We'll be there, Ramón."

"My wife's sister is a doctor. You know how many sisters my wife got? Four. All of them crazy." He looked at me. "Fast. When my baby starts knocking I must drive fast."

"We'll need proof of residency and your original birth certificates," said Octavian. "Also, I'll ask you to formalize the retainer now. Your payment of the retainer legally authorizes me to act on your behalf. The rest of the money, you can pay after you receive your son's Canadian passport. If you want we can meet you at your apartment."

"Don't be crazy. The whole CDR will be watching. I'll drop your friend here off in front of the resort and I'll give you the money in the car park. Shake my hand. Make it look like a tip."

"I already gave you a tip," I said.

"You do know that what we're doing is entirely legal, don't you?" said Octavian.

"Everything here is illegal. If it's not permitted, it's illegal. Do as I say," said Ramón.

Relieved that he wasn't angry anymore, I put out my hand. "We're all on board, Ramón. I'm glad. What made you change your mind? Is it because you figured out that maybe, just maybe, we're not devils after all?"

"No," said Ramón still smiling but colder now. "It's because we're desperate."

He dropped me off by the patio. I donned sunglasses and pretended to flip through a magazine, but through the corner of my eye I could see Ramón's hand hovering over an envelope. His thumb clung to it, reluctant to let go, and I saw him follow it with his eyes even after Octavian had folded the envelope away into his own pocket. It was probably the most money Ramón had ever held at one time in his whole life. It was probably all of the bribe money he had ever fiddled. But we took it just the same.

Chapter 7
The Maternity Boat

When the Peugeot had safely vanished from sight, Octavian joined me on the patio and we discreetly shook hands. I noted with satisfaction that his palms were damp.

"That was intense," I said. "And what was he talking about? What's a CDR?"

Octavian snorted. "It means *Committee for the Defence of the Revolution*. The local neighbourhood spy network. Enough now. I require dinner. The Italian restaurant at this resort is a match for any trattoria in Rome. We can toast the future dominance of the Castro and Roger Professional Legal Corporation. Mags can join us, if we can pry him out of his wife."

When we got back to our room there were strange shuffling noises emanating from within.

"Typical third-world thieves," said Octavian, more bored than alarmed. He rapped on the door. "Come on out, criminals. Either that or jump to your deaths."

Something from the vicinity of the room emitted a high-pitched yelp, but there was no one in sight but the cleaning lady, who nodded to us over her mop and said "Hola." We looked at each other and Octavian pushed open the door.

Marycarmen was stretched on a bed – Octavian's bed – lithe and pouting barefoot in a white bikini and high heels. When she saw me she squealed and threw her arms around my neck. "My flight was overbooked," she lisped. "So they put me on an earlier one. I was just trying on my bathing suit."

"Wow," I said, putting my hands on the warm springy flesh of her hips and kissing her. "It looks – wow. We were on our way to dinner, did you want to – wow."

"I would love to get dinner," she purred.

"How did you get into our room?" said Octavian irritably. "This is private property, Marycarmen, and it's illegal to break and enter."

"I didn't break and enter," said Marycarmen, pouting even harder. "Don't be so mean, Octavian. I just asked the man at the desk to let me into my boyfriend's room and he said sure. Okay Walter, I need to show you something. You've seen the white one. Remember what it looks like, okay?" She freed herself of my embrace, dashed into the bathroom and reappeared almost instantaneously in a scanty gold contraption that seemed to be tied at her belly button in a tantalizing bow. One pull and the whole thing would unravel.

"What do you think?" she said. "This one or the white one?"

"Definitely the gold one," I said, trying to hold her again, but she moved at the last second and I ended up with a mouthful of fragrant hair.

"Octavian, what about you?" she said, to no reply.

"What about dinner?" I said, but she had flounced off, undulating her bottom, paralyzing every male in her radius except one. Mags was blithely tripping down the hall in his short purple caftan, a sleeping white-blond child clinging to him like a limpet.

"Hola, Walter. Octavian. How did it work out today?"

"That was my girlfriend. Look but don't touch, buddy."

"Who, the cleaning lady? Good for you, man. Score. Listen, I was asking the waitress at lunch about places to visit in the area and the only thing she could say was 'La Habana'." He affected a high female voice with a Cuban accent. "'La Habana so wonderful. La Habana so beautiful'. Maxine was thinking that maybe we should take a trip out there tomorrow. Maybe we can steal John Lennon's glasses for one of the kids."

"Havana is a dump," said Octavian briefly. "You're not going anywhere, Mags. We need you. It just so happens that we have sealed the deal with our client."

"Havana's supposed to be the jewel of the Caribbean. The cathedral. The capitol building. And all he can say is 'Old Havana is a dump'. It can't be a dump. I've seen pictures of the San Cristobal Cathedral. It's magnificent."

"Our clients don't live in the cathedral, Mags. They live with Ramón's sister and her five children in a two-bedroom apartment near the Malecón. I like Ramón. It's not just the money, I want to help him. I've got copies of the boat's registration. Have you started on the registrar's certificate? It needs to be notarized."

"It's done."

"Why? You didn't even know if the client committed or not."

"I did it for fun. Maxine was taking a nap. I can give you the stack of documents now if you want; most of them are notarized. Even though failure is guaranteed, I'm almost looking forward to dumping this brick on the bureaucrats at the embassy, just to watch them squirm their way out of it. Don't ask me to notarize anything else though, the kids got into it and now I'm out of stamping ink. On the bright side, they've notarized all of their colouring books."

Octavian smiled broadly and clapped him on the shoulder. "Nice work. This should get you a Queen's Counsel at least. Let's have dinner, you uxorious bastard."

"Maxine and I already ate at the tapas restaurant. She's getting her nails done now."

"So eat twice. You look bulimic. Are you bulimic?"

"Yes," said Mags defiantly. "I have had bulimic episodes. Mental illness isn't a crime, okay Octavian?"

"Excellent," said Octavian. "So we all have empty stomachs."

The restaurant was tucked away behind red-checked curtains in a brick façade at the back of the main complex. Inside it was softly illuminated by tall red candles that flickered on each table. A hostess in heavy eye-shadow and a black bow tie ushered us to the bar, where I spotted Marycarmen, bewitching by candlelight, though unusually conservative in a long black skirt.

"That's my girl," I said to Mags. "Baby misses me. Watch. She's going to light up like a Christmas tree when she sees me."

"Look who's with her, idiot," said Octavian softly, and when I looked again I saw that Marycarmen was flanked by a pair of thickset Mexicans, one male in a brown suit and one female wearing the biggest crucifix I had ever seen.

"Who the hell are they?" I said.

"Her parents, obviously," said Octavian. "Do you have parents in your culture?"

"You cheated on the cleaning lady?" said Mags.

The hawk eyes of the man who was probably Marycarmen's father seemed to rest on us for a second. Then he stood up and beckoned us over.

"Who, me?" I mouthed.

"Yes you!" he shouted, to the consternation of the entire restaurant. "Yes, you! You, the takeout-restaurant lawyers! I know all about you! I want to know which one of you has corrupted my daughter!" Bravely I tried to bolt for the door, but Octavian had an iron grip on my wrist. The man looked at me and howled at Marycarmen, "This? This *pendejo* you have chosen? Why could you at least not choose the handsome one for your debauchery? He is at least Mexican!" He took a step back and squinted uncertainly. "I think."

"Papa, I swear to you I do not have any boyfriend –"

"José, quietly," whispered the mother.

"Look!" yelled the father, pointing to the limpet that still clung sleepily to Mags, and he poured forth a stream of Spanish before switching to English for the big finish. "Look what pain she has given us. She told us she has come here for a practicum! Look at our bastard grandchild! That is your practicum!"

Marycarmen was weeping now, rocking back and forth, and everyone in the restaurant had paused their suppers to watch the show. Even the hostess in the velvet bow tie was staring open-mouthed. Marycarmen looked at me with swollen pleading eyes. I shrugged helplessly, but Octavian stepped forward and said something in Spanish that made Marycarmen stop crying and the father turn red.

"Leave me to deal with this. Mags, please meet me first thing in the morning," he said tiredly. "Walter, you're a despicable human being."

ඉ

I probably was a despicable human being: by any measure of affection I ought to have dreamed of Marycarmen that night. Instead I dreamed of Ramón. My mother had probably told me half a dozen times since I'd started working for Octavian that it was perfectly normal for men to dream of other men, and there certainly were erotic elements to the dream, but my primary sensation was guilt. Ramón was a superior man to me in every way. He was strong and young and beautiful. He drove fast. He supported families; he had sired a child. I still asked my mother for pocket money. Ramón drank books for lunch, yet he had reached the apex of his career in Havana. In Cuba he wouldn't ever be anything more than another petty official on the take, steadily less handsome, and one day someone would probably knife him.

When I awoke it was morning. Octavian was lying on his back naked in the adjacent bed. He was still as a statue but his eyes were wide open in the morning Caribbean sun.

"Hey buddy," I said, turning over. "How did it go last night?"

"Congratulations Walter," he said. "You're engaged to Marycarmen."

"What?"

"You heard me, amigo."

I leapt over to his bed like some kind of panther and landed squarely on his crotch.

Octavian looked up at me, unperturbed by the sudden sexuality of the situation. "I thought you loved her. My girlfriend this and my girlfriend that. Now you'll be with your girlfriend forever."

Of course my rational brain knew that I couldn't physically be forced to marry anyone, but I also knew that Marycarmen's father was a man easily capable of killing me to death. "I don't know what you've negotiated with those terrorists, Octavian, but I'm not marrying Marycarmen, not now, not ever. I barely know her. Her father had a gun!"

Octavian sat up to face me so that our noses were almost touching, and I could see that there were huge bags under his eyes. "I'm joking," he said. "One of us is engaged to that stupid girl, though, and unfortunately it's me."

"Thanks, man," I said, sliding relieved off of his crotch.

"I didn't do it for you, you selfish prick. Didn't you see how she was crying?"

"She cried so hard you're going to marry her. If I married every woman who cried at me I'd have at least two wives by now, including my mother. What do you care, man? Are you trying to show me up? You were cheating on her." I tossed a hotel dressing gown at him. "And could you cover up please? I'm not homophobic but this situation is getting needlessly gay."

He threw the gown across the room with surprising violence. "We have two clients counting on us to get them out of Cuba. I have Mags here on high alert. I've got two video shoots on the backburner in Miami and every second of delay is costing me piles of money. When we get back to Toronto I'll quietly break it off with Marycarmen and you can do whatever you want, just stay away from her while we're in Cuba. You owe me big time for this, Walter. Your take just got a lot smaller."

"Where's Marycarmen now?"

His eyes were fixed to the ceiling. "Who the hell knows? Who the hell cares? All I know is that they're not leaving. Your dumb girlfriend told them she was here for a nursing practicum. I should never have allowed either of you to set foot in Cuba. But it's too late now and you're all stuck to me like leeches. I really thought she would kill herself."

"She's not even really my girlfriend yet. Physically, if you know what I mean."

"Do you think I don't know that? You couldn't be more obviously impotent. You brought her here. As soon as the going got tough you sold her to the lowest bidder. You're not a man. A man takes care of his own."

Octavian insulted me constantly, but there was no trace of mirth in this latest pronouncement.

"I'm not a man, then. And you are, is that what you're trying to tell me? You try being a man with my kind of debt and no job. We've all got to eat, brother, and not all of us have rich daddies," was what came out of my mouth.

"We've all got to eat. You think you have it so hard. Ramón and Estella, now they have it hard."

"But you still took their money, didn't you? Don't be a hypocrite, Octavian. I'm leaving now. I'm not missing out on a free breakfast because of you."

Octavian sat up on the bed. "You do that, you fat tub. Eat up. Eat everything in sight. Because as soon as we get back to Toronto we are finished. You're a garbage lawyer and a garbage human being."

I slammed the door, hard. On my way to the breakfast room, Estella waved from at the concierge's desk, her red hair almost as voluminous as her belly.

"Where is your handsome friend?"

"He isn't my friend," I said brightly. "He's my colleague."

She lowered her voice. "My husband has told me everything. My husband says that you are men of your words. He says you are men with high morality."

"Are you sure he said that?"

"Oh yes," she said. She touched her stomach and beamed, and I felt my own stomach churn a little. "You are great men."

"Thanks. Lots to do today," I said briskly, and pushing her heart-shaped smile out of my mind I marched purposefully into the breakfast room, where the usual slate of Germans methodically chomped their way through the morning's nutrition. There was also a new, unwelcome party: Marycarmen and family. The parents were sitting at a back table sipping tea in the sunshine, looking infinitely more pleasant than they had the night before. Marycarmen was in line for the buffet. Fortunately she was in front of an obvious Canadian, so I cut in line to join her, the man behind me betraying only the faintest of passive-aggressive sighs as I accidentally trod on his foot.

"Oh, hi Walter," she said nicely.

"I missed you, Carmenita," I said into her ear. "I've been

thinking about the fashion show you gave me yesterday. You're quite the little supermodel, aren't you?"

She blushed. "Come on, Walter. That's all in the past now. I'm with Octavian now and this time it's forever."

"In the past? It was yesterday! What about me? Was it all a game?"

"Walter, please. You walked away yesterday. You didn't even say goodbye."

"I just want to know if I ever meant anything to you."

"Octavian never cared about anyone but me, Walter. We're soulmates. We all knew that in our hearts all along. My parents forgave Octavian and we're going to be married."

"They forgave Octavian for what? If Octavian owes anyone an apology, it's me!"

"Aww, thanks, Walter. You're so sweet." Then she turned her attention to the selection of juices.

She wanted Octavian, then. It was always Octavian. I watched her bend over the croissants in her silky skirts – long and demure now that her parents were in evidence – with a wincing pain in my chest. There were seventy-five people docilely chewing cheese hunks in the room, and their mastication sounds made me want to hit something. Instead I seized an entire intact platter of cold meats and carried it to my own corner of the room, gnawing down on the contents like a wild animal.

Octavian cantered in shortly afterward. He'd changed and washed and brushed, and he calmly joined his new pretend family at the breakfast table as though it was the most natural thing in the world to propose marriage to your partner's girlfriend. Marycarmen beamed up at him, hanging adoringly on every word he uttered, and I even caught the grey-haired double that was Marycarmen's mother smiling a little as she looked on at the young couple in fake love.

I shovelled the few remaining meat tendons left on my plate into my mouth. On my way back to our room I collided with Mags, who now sported a tiny bump of beer-bloat in place of his formerly concave stomach.

"Hola, Walter," he said. "Where's Octavian? Estella's about to pop any second. Trust me on that, I'm an expert. We need to get to that boat."

"Why don't you just go and puke up your breakfast, you male bulimic?" I rapped out, but there was no unseating the new, serene Mags.

"I haven't eaten yet," he said cheerfully. "And do you know what? Cuba really agrees with me. I've barely felt like vomiting at all. Hey, aren't you coming? I ran into Marycarmen's parents this morning and they invited me to breakfast."

So everyone was invited to the happy couple's impromptu engagement party except me. That was it, then. I needed to leave the resort before the rage simmering in my belly erupted into something worse. I stamped back to our room and directly ransacked Octavian's suitcase. He'd packed it like a professional laundress, with layers of tissue paper between his fine silk shirts, and I took a deep pleasure in crushing it until my fingers closed upon a roll of bills tamped neatly into a sock. It was Ramón's retainer; it had been Octavian's for a while, but now it was mine, just like Marycarmen had been. I took the money and threw the sock into the toilet. Then I sprinted out in the direction of the taxi stand. The taxi driver would know what to do. Taxi drivers were men of the world.

I'd never solicited a prostitute before – I'd never knowingly even met one – but I had the notion that Cuba might be an excellent place to try it. And why not? I deserved some fun, and Cuba was rife with pretty girls like the ones who'd obviously craved me on the Malecón. I hadn't been born with a silver spoon up my sphincter like Octavian had, and if nothing else, a Cuban girl would probably be cheaper than the fat bundle I'd wasted on Marycarmen's plane ticket. A taxi rounded the driveway and pulled up to the stand – a new Kia – and I climbed in, sweating hard with my own resolve, but the words *do you know any nice girls around here* turned to vinegar on my tongue: the driver was either the same monosyllabic, road-raging delight of two nights before, or his precise clone. He shoved the taxi into the entrance of a surprisingly modern and upscale-looking shopping mall, ripped the fare from my hand and whizzed away in his squeaking Kia. Fantastic. Even I knew you couldn't buy a prostitute at a shopping mall, and the place was half empty anyway except for a few Russian tourists barking at each other in their terrifying language. Outside the mall there were no road signs or billboards or traffic lights, only wide, dusty roads dotted with palm trees and a few skittery cars.

The way to do it, probably, was to gravitate away from the high-gloss, tourist-friendly centre and find the scummy bits of the town: the drug-dealers and the car-stealers, the black-market shills and dispensers of pills. Would it really be such a bad thing? I was a nice guy, a respectable lawyer, good to my mother, or at the very least civil; I worked hard at my job, I'd showered affection on Marycarmen, who had pretended every kiss, every caress, from the very beginning. I wasn't seeking a child or a transsexual or a cripple in a wheelchair. Why was it so wrong to pay for the company of a beautiful woman? I would buy her a meal, pay for her drinks, take her for a pleasant swim, and if it led to more, then well, who was I to deny a woman what she wanted? The slogan *It's a free country, isn't it?* flitted into my brain before I remembered that, despite the best efforts of the Cuban Ministry of Tourism to make me forget it, I was not in Canada, I was in Cuba, which was adamantly not a free country. At the very least it was less free than mine.

I started walking in no particular direction in the already blistering noontime heat, past a single *turista* restaurant thatched with straw and a few squat little three-storey apartment blocks with all of the windows shuttered. I had no particular destination in mind and merely followed the gradient of steepest ugliness. The roads remained the same, wide and dusty without any traffic lights or signage, but the buildings steadily got smaller and more worn, strewn with old concrete blocks, fallen shingles and patches of yellow scrub grass. Aside from a few women in slippers and housedresses standing in line at the counter of what was ostensibly a shop

– it was hard to tell, there was almost nothing on the shelves behind the counter – there was no one in sight, never mind the parade of cheap and cheerful streetwalkers greeting me with Cuban flags and pitchers of sangria that had filled my daydreams in the taxi from the Cabos Melia.

In the distance I could see the ocean sparkling, and for lack of any better ideas I walked all the way down to the water's edge. Perhaps I would find some kind of novel aquatic Cuban mermaid hooker. Unlike the Cabos Melia, with its pristine powdery sands and orderly rows of sun-beds, the beach here was uncombed, brown and strewn with dead jellyfish, empty except for a lonely couple walking hand-in-hand on the jetty. It was a romantic-looking tableau and I had a quick, sharp pang of jealousy until I looked a little bit closer. The man was white – mottled pink, actually – and easily sixty or sixty-five years old, in a blue T-shirt stretched taut over a soft paunch. The girl – and she was very much a girl, not a day over twenty – was kicking stones into the water. She was a Cuban with a mass of springy dark curls and an admirably reed-like body in cut-off denim shorts.

The man apparently caught me watching her, and despite the distance between us I could clearly see him wink through his round-rimmed spectacles. It was a smirk-wink, the wink of a man raising his palm for a high-five, and I winked right back at him, in part because the girl's beauty merited some form of response, but mostly because I am a monkey. I noticed that he had a rather full head of grey-white hair, something that I was inclined to notice now that my own was thinning a little in front. The girl kicked another stone into the water, showing a long swath of skinny brown leg.

It only occurred to me then that he was probably paying for her company. Of course, I had instinctively recognized something odd about the situation – couples mismatched in attractiveness are often mismatched in other ways as well – usually wealth – but I suppose that my brain wasn't overeager to recognize itself in the smug old man with a fatty liver taking his granddaughter for a walk.

I might have assumed that the pair of them, the hooker and her satisfied customer, would have seen the benefit of keeping their arrangement discreet – prostitution is definitely illegal in Cuba – but they stepped off the jetty, still arm-in-arm, and aimed themselves in my direction.

"Hello there, sir," said the man politely when they were in earshot. My heart sank a little as I realized that he had the accent of a fellow Canadian, and probably an educated one as well; apparently we were a nation of university-going whoremongers.

"You from Canada?" he said.

"Toronto," I said.

"I'm from outside of Toronto. You know Napanee? It's near Kingston."

"I know Kingston, sure. My buddy Patrick lives there."

"How do you like Cuba so far? This your first visit?"

"Yep, my first time. It beats the winter, that's for sure."

"The food's not great, but for this kind of sunshine, who cares?"

"So true, so true."

"I'm Bill," said the man, extending a hand. "I want you to meet my girlfriend Mariela. Say hi, Mariela."

"Hi," said the girl called Mariela, high and clear and almost unbearably childish. She waved one of her hands; the other was tucked into the back pocket of her lover's shorts.

"This is my eighth visit," said the man who called himself Bill. "You know, not a lot of tourists come to this part of Varadero. Can I ask what brings you here?"

I looked away. "Nothing, just taking a walk –"

"Are you looking for a girlfriend?" he said courteously.

Of course I was, and as I watched slim-hipped Mariela smile and simper a little bit, winding her ringlets around her finger, my lust for a girlfriend of any kind only multiplied, but I couldn't bring myself to admit it to this man.

"You can have one for thirty bucks," said Bill. His frankness alarmed me and I looked at Mariela, who said nothing. "For another ten you can stay at her place and she'll probably even cook for you. It's actually a better deal than the resort," he added helpfully, like a man giving directions, and suddenly I was filled with shame. I looked at Mariela again, but her face remained smooth, impassive, even cheerful.

"Don't you worry about Mariela here," he said. "She doesn't speak much English. She doesn't need to, if you get my drift. But I think we understand each other pretty well. Don't we, sweetheart?" he said, tilting the girl towards him and kissing her face with his lizard lips, which she received without flinching. He was showing off now and I liked him even less for it.

"That's great," I said. "Well, thanks for the tip."

But he was unable to contain himself. "One girl did it for a pair of shoes. I swear she was sixteen years old."

"That's great, man," I said, openly sarcastic now, and I turned to leave but he stopped me with his free hand.

"Hey there," he said, apparently wounded and tightening his grip around Mariela, "don't get the wrong idea. These girls want it. Not like the women back home, feminist bitches one and all. I never would have even come here if it hadn't been for my ex-wife cleaning me out. Sex is like the national sport on this island. Do you think any girl in her right mind would do it for just a pair of shoes? Hell no. She wanted something else, do you get my drift?"

"Sorry, Bill, I need to get back to my friends –"

"Do you want Mariela here to give you a kiss? Mariela, give my friend here a little kiss."

She looked away, still saying nothing.

"Oh come on. I won't look." He turned and covered his eyes with exaggerated care.

Mariela didn't look at him. She stalked over to me, wound her arms around my waist, and gave me a hot, dry, and surprisingly hard kiss. When she finished my heart was pounding.

Bill uncovered his eyes. "How did you like that, buddy?"

I looked at his candid, expectant face and backed away from them as quickly as I could, retracing my steps back to the

Varadero mall – still strangely shuttered and empty except for the company of barking Russians. I might have gone to Havana and sought the company of the *jineteras* by the Malecón, but Mariela had killed my appetite for prostitutes, although I wasn't precisely sure why. Prostitution was as legitimate as any other business, I supposed. Back home prostitutes probably weren't prostitutes at all, but "sexual satisfaction associates" or some such, and as Canadians they were probably all unionized. No, it was her automaton obedience as her hands slid down my waist, that and the man's white liver-spotted hands on the girl's milk chocolate skin; sex was a monopoly of the young, and in the natural world a pretty girl like poor Mariela, scarcely younger than I was, rightfully ought to have chosen me, not him, only I hadn't thought to pack her a pair of shoes.

In the mall, the same mahogany-coloured taxi driver was smoking cross-eyed in the parking lot. He inspected me through the windshield of his Kia as I checked my phone to find a litany of wrathful missives from Mags. Just my luck: Estella had gone into labour. I could practically hear Octavian sneering.

"Marina Hemingway please," I said, to the back of the driver's dank skull.

He turned around. "What for?"

"I'm meeting friends," I said, and to passive-aggressively inform him that I was in no mood to converse I climbed into his car, leaned back, closed my eyes and emitted a grotesque snore. I suppose he got the message, because he flipped the radio station to Radio Havana Cuba and in very little time at all the hard Spanish prattle with its harsh *r* sounds, so meaningless to me, lulled me to sleep.

I awoke to a huge pair of bug eyes peering at me upside-down and a blaring T-shirt that read *EPTECH 19th Annual Electronic Trade Show Volunteer*. A fingernail descended and flicked me in the face.

"Mags?" I said, as my eyes came into focus.

"Where the hell have you been? Estella went into labour hours ago," said Mags shortly. He pulled me roughly out of the Kia into the blinking sun and the fish-salt smell of the beach. The second my feet touched the ground, the taxi jerked forward and screamed away, vanishing in less than four seconds without so much as a backward glance from the driver.

"Hurry up."

"Come on Mags. Don't be upset."

"You're late. Late to the sole reason for our trip. Unbelievable."

Down on the dock a well-oiled olive-skinned figure in blue bathing trunks emerged from one of the boats and squinted up in our direction. It was Octavian, and he was waving a briefcase. "Mags!" he shouted. "Hurry up please, it's time!"

"It's show time, I'd better run," said Mags, tearing down the hill on his skinny bowlegs.

I followed him down onto the dock, where the promised boat stood bobbing with Octavian at the helm and the words *Cuba Libre* embossed on the side in gold. I knew exactly nought about boats, but even I could see that it was easily the most handsome craft on the dock, a sleek two-level affair with a wide deck and a nose tapered like that of a swordfish.

Octavian studied me as I clambered onto the deck. His bare chest was luminescent with sunscreen. "Thief," he said. "I have no more respect for you. Where's the money you stole?"

"Alright, Octavian," I said wearily. "Take it. Half of it is my money anyway. Where's Marycarmen?"

"Don't start, Casanova, and kindly remove your grubby fingers from my person, I don't have any pockets in these shorts," said Octavian. "She's down in the cabin helping the doctor, so just leave her the hell alone. I'll take the money later."

"Protecting our territory, are we?" I sneered, the violence in my stomach swelling again, and I forced myself to look away from him.

Ramón's dark, perspiring head emerged from below the deck. "Oh, it's you," he said briefly to me. "Octavian, *asere*, have you got any more of that rum?"

Octavian smiled slightly and produced a bottle and two shot glasses from his briefcase. Ramón drank them both. He closed his eyes and leaned against the hull for a moment. "You're a good lawyer, Octavian. The best," and held out his glass again.

"Hi Ramón," I said. "Can I ask what's taking so long down there?"

Mags groaned from his post on the deck and Ramón's face darkened. "This guy. A clown, hey? You want a punch in the face?" Then he changed his mind. "Walter, don't listen to me. The pressure is great. You want to be godfather to my child?"

"Well, I'm not sure that −"

"I'm a joker. I'm joking you. My brother will be the godfather. My wife, her entire family is down there, you saw them, Mr. Magellan, they're driving me to an early grave. Oh, and I like your nurse. A beauty. Okay, I'm going back to Dante's inferno now."

"Hey Mags," said Octavian, bored as ever. "Don't look so happy. For a change it's not yours."

"That's exactly why I'm so happy," said Mags, patting a specimen of his own genetic output, which was fast asleep in the sunshine. "That and the fact that it's time for some serious lawyering. Let's give them an hour to get the kid cleaned up and then we'll go and get everything signed."

But apparently Ramón was having none of that. Not even forty minutes had elapsed before he called up to us on the deck. "Hey! Lawyers! Canadian lawyers! Come here now and greet my Canadian son!"

None of us particularly hankered to meet his Canadian son, or smell the afterbirth of his Cuban wife, but we tramped downstairs anyway into the ship's berth, a narrow wood-panelled affair where Octavian and Mags were greeted like returning heroes by the conclave of relatives. One of the women − Estella's older sister, probably, judging by the pouf of red hair − gave me a hard stare.

"Ramón," she bellowed, "Let me get this straight. Your wife gives you a son and the first person you call is another lawyer? What's the matter with you?"

Ramón waved her away and said something in Spanish

that made everyone laugh. In English he said, "When my son goes to Canada he can thank his lucky stars he doesn't have to listen to this woman ever again. Hey, there's Señorita Marycarmen."

Marycarmen emerged from the cabin. Her black hair was damp and her face was flushed with huge dark circles under her eyes, but in her arms she clutched the key to the whole affair: a small, moist squirming thing that was unmistakeably a baby. She gave me a careless smile, and I tasted bile in my throat; it was her fault, the whole smarmy business in Varadero, me sniffing for whores like a disoriented hound dog.

"You keep looking at her that way, and soon you'll be a papa too," advised the older sister. "You want to see little Ernesto, or what?"

I opened my mouth to tell her that I did not, but she yelled something in Spanish and the wrinkled raisin of a child was passed from hand to hand until finally he landed in my arms. I was uncertain of how to hold him, and not at all impressed by the beauty of his wet scarlet face. Nonetheless I felt a strange sort of paternal attachment to this dark-haired imp, whom fate and a little ineptitude had brought into the world on a seafaring vessel, nominally a Canadian military ship, somewhere in a sleepy port in the middle of the Caribbean Sea. I took a breath and stroked his tiny, soft little fingers.

"Welcome to Canada," I said dubiously.

Chapter 8
Soliciting

We evacuated the boat the very same day, and I have to say I felt sorry for poor Estella, who looked as haggard as death in some kind of a clean white wrapper, clutching her abdomen as she staggered up the narrow wooden stairs to the deck, supported by two more of her innumerable sisters. Ramón carried the baby behind her like a priest in a church processional. The pouf-haired older sister solemnly shook hands with Marycarmen and followed them out to the marina where Ramón's brother was waiting with the car.

Almost instantly after they left, another car pulled up on the hillside and discharged two round, brown, scowling Mexicans in shirtsleeves and crosses: Marycarmen's parents, whom I hadn't missed in the slightest. When Marycarmen saw them she groaned.

"There are your folks. So long, Marycarmen," said Octavian.

"What, you're leaving?" The words leaked out of my mouth before I could stop them.

"You can only take three days off for a practicum, Walter. I've got an exam tomorrow." She turned back to Octavian. "I'm going to miss you so much, *mi amor*. You know, I always thought I'd be so scared of giving birth, but after seeing Estella tonight I felt the power of being a woman. One day I'm going to give you a baby."

Octavian gingerly patted her hair.

"Hey! Down, boy! Save something for the wedding night," said Marycarmen's mother, waddling up between them and ignoring me entirely. "How are you, dearie? Handsome as ever?" she said to Octavian, who winced.

The father came directly to me with his hand outstretched. "I am very, very sorry, son," he said. "About last night, the fault was all mine. When you become a father you will understand what it is to feel so deeply for your child that you are ready to kill on her behalf. Nonetheless what I said to you was not excusable and I ask your forgiveness."

"It's quite alright, sir," I said, feeling a little sorry for him as a vision of his precious daughter, hot and panting in the office closet, popped into my head. Marycarmen looked on serenely. It was astonishing how completely she took my complicity in her sex games for granted.

The man made a slight bow. "Come, Marycarmen. If she has completed her practicum, then it is time for us to take her home. She has an exam tomorrow. It was very nice to meet you again, Mr. Roger."

"Likewise, sir, madam. Bye, Marycarmen," I said.

"Bye, Walter," she sang.

The sun was beginning to set in a blaze of orange over the sea. Mags poured us shots of rum.

"What a shame we have to leave this boat," mused Octavian. "It's magnificent, isn't it?"

"If we get a few more clients you can buy your own boat," I said. "You won't have to borrow Scarface's anymore."

"There won't be any more clients," said Mags, killing joy at his usual breakneck speed. "After the pen pushers fire-bomb your application the feds will shut the loophole and throw away the key."

"Probably they will," allowed Octavian. "But government moves about as fast as a herd of snails. We'll push through a thousand applications exactly like this one before the fourth deputy minister can say 'let's form an exploratory committee'. Believe me, Professor Magtastic, this gig will keep us in rum and boats for a while."

Octavian and I set off the very next day for the Canadian embassy with a sealed briefcase of documents. Ramón insisted on driving us. We waited for him in the Cabos Melia lobby attired in the biggest, boxiest, most intimidating lawyer suits we possessed. Mags waited with us, still in his peekaboo caftan – apparently it was the only article of clothing he possessed –

serenely slurping strawberry juice from a champagne flute.

"Cheer up, Octavian. You look like death warmed over. You should just be thankful the mother and baby made it out of there alive and kicking," advised Mags. "It's the first rule of lawyering. First, create no liabilities."

"It's his fake engagement to my girlfriend," I said. "Selling out your partner is high stress. Although I wouldn't know, of course. I would never do that to a friend."

"We're not friends," said Octavian mildly.

"Focus on the positive," insisted Mags. He proffered the tray of goodies he'd been bringing to his wife. "Both of you have a drink. Let's make a toast."

Octavian nodded and raised a cup of orange juice. "To the loophole," he said. I toasted with the only liquid left on the tray, a pitcher of milk.

"The loophole," I agreed.

"To me," said Mags, gulping from his champagne flute. "It was my idea. People are always profiting from my ideas. And I'll thank you to remember that when payday comes."

"No way. You had your chance," said Octavian, and for once I agreed with him.

"Just remember you're not out of the woods yet. Not even close. Half the people at the embassy won't know what *jus soli* means, and the other half will have never heard of a citizenship certificate," said Mags.

To get him off his high horse I showed him a bracelet I'd bought in Varadero. "It's a souvenir for my mom. Nice, eh?"

"No, it's garbage, probably made in China. You should have gotten her something authentic."

"What did you want me to get her, a lifetime membership in the Communist party of Cuba?"

"Come on. He's here," said Octavian sharply.

"Adios and good luck," said Mags, giving his champagne flute a final disgusting lick before tripping back to his family with a much depleted tray.

Ramón was quieter, more subdued this time as he glided the Peugeot out of the grand circle of the Cabos Melia's driveway en route to Havana.

"How's little Ernesto?" said Octavian.

Ramón bowed, insofar as the steering wheel would allow it. "Baby is good. Strong. My boy grabs your finger, he won't let go. Where is Mr. Magellan today?" He seemed to have conceived an exaggerated respect for Mags. I should have told him that he needn't have bothered: no one else did.

"He's not necessary for this part of the operation," said Octavian smoothly.

"How's your wife?" I said.

"Yeah, good. I dunno. Her mother and sisters are in the house. Day, night, blah, blah, talk, talk."

"Women," I said, his comrade in masculine contempt as I thought bitterly of Marycarmen.

Ramón snapped, "Listen, that's my wife you're talking about," and shut his mouth for the next hundred kilometres.

Octavian was silent.

"Octavian, *asere*, what's the matter with you?" asked Ramón abruptly. "You've got troubles?"

Octavian's head jerked up. "Not at all. Not at all, Ramón. I've just been thinking about how to frame our arguments to the embassy people."

"Arguments, there's no argument," said Ramón. "If it's the law, it's the law. That's the difference between Cuba and Canada. In Canada the law is the law. You've got human rights. My son is a Canadian because that's the law."

The green gaze was too intense. Octavian and I looked away from the rear-view mirror and eyed each other uneasily. Ramón suffered from one of the prime afflictions of the less developed world: rose-tinted goggles. The foreign officials who floated in and out of his Ministry served as his binoculars and through them he peered into North America, and everything he saw there was beautiful and good.

"The law is the law," agreed Octavian. "But there are no guarantees when you deal with bureaucrats. You know that better than anyone."

"Of course. Now that you have my money there are no

guarantees."

The car suddenly sped up and swerved dangerously. "Take it easy. You're not a bachelor anymore," Octavian said.

We were deep in Havana now, in the thick of city traffic, a mix of French and Korean cars, mopeds, "coco taxis" – hollow plastic shells in which the passengers rattled about like peanuts – and big vintage American cars creaking on what remained of their axles. Pedestrians crossed willy-nilly as the mood struck them, and Ramón dodged them like bullets. When he pulled up alongside the red-roofed Canadian embassy in Miramar he turned around. His face was red.

"I'll be outside waiting. If you don't see me, just keep waiting. My son is a Canadian now. That means he's one of your people. So you take care of him, hey, lawyers? I have given you my trust. Also my money."

"Take it easy," advised Octavian, and gently closed the door.

The embassy was remarkable for its Canadian flag, the mess of satellite dishes on its otherwise flat red roof, and the fact that unlike its neighbours, the Spanish-style building was still in a reasonable state of repair, with fresh white paint on its stone façade. Even without these attributes it still would have been one of the most conspicuous places in Havana. Humans of both sexes looped around the building in a sweaty ribbon, fighting for territory and fanning themselves. We wound our way around the queue and planted ourselves at the end of it. For the next four hours we limped toward the main doors, one person and two steps at a time, until finally we stood at the front of the line.

ℚℚ

"No."

We were sitting in an office that was small and pink with a thick crack running down the back wall. Seated low behind a desk that spanned nearly the entire width of the room was a man who was also pink and small, with a brown moustache that looked like a rat taped to his face. The man's name tag read "Derek Walcott, Consular Assistant" and he was shaking his head with the charisma of a filing cabinet.

"What do you mean, no?" said Octavian, who had scrunched himself in his chair to minimize his own height and handsomeness. "I've explained the situation in full. I grant that the circumstances are unusual, but all of the paperwork is in order, Mr. Walcott. We have ample evidence attesting to the circumstances of little Ernesto Iguarez Flores's birth. He was born to my clients on a Canadian military ship."

"There are no military ships in the vicinity. Not unless we invaded Cuba and no one told me about it." The sad corners of Derek Walcott's mouth turned vaguely upward. It had been a joke. So I laughed.

Octavian laughed even louder. "Heaven forbid, sir. It wasn't your standard military ship, I grant you that. We're employing the definition of military ship as it is set out in the *Canadian Naval War Act, R.S. 1937*. I have three copies of the act for you in my briefcase, with the relevant parts highlighted, but if you'd like to double-check for yourself, I see you have a copy of the federal statutes right there behind you on your shelf."

"We don't process citizenship here," said Walcott, and it occurred to me that he was the male version of the android who was my old classmate Kristen, except without Kristen's robust masculinity. "It's not our policy. We process work visas, tourist visas, regular and commercial immigration. If your clients are Cuban residents with no family connections to Canada, then there is no possible direct path to citizenship. Tell them to start with a permanent residency application. I tell people that three, four times a week but I have to say it's the first time I've ever had to say it to a lawyer. A foreign national has to do a lot more for Canadian citizenship than just ask for it. Okay, gentlemen? See Angel on your way out and he'll give you some forms."

"I hear you, Mr. Walcott. It's been a long day. I'd love nothing more than to waltz out of here and go to the beach," I said.

"But we have an obligation to our clients," said Octavian. "You can't decline an application without even looking at it, sir."

The man gave him a tight little smile. "It's at my discretion, sir."

"It isn't, I'm afraid," said Octavian, not smiling anymore. "This isn't a visa application. If you accept the circumstances of Ernesto Iguarez Flores's birth, then citizenship flows by matter of right, not discretion. It's that simple."

Walcott's eyebrows shot up to his hairline. His hand retreated from the desk and moved to his belly, which he began to massage with long strokes. "I think I'll be the judge of that."

"Fine," said Octavian. "You're the judge. What's your verdict?"

Walcott looked pained. He stared at his watch. He looked at a conch-shell paperweight on his desk. He looked at the crack on the wall. A crude plaster repair job had been effected in some bygone century and two giant maps had been taped over its obvious failure: one of Cuba and one of Canada, each flanked by a framed photograph of its leader. After he had thoroughly examined every feature of the room he gave a queasy-smelling sigh and said: "Today of all days."

"We have notarized birth certificates for both parents, copies of all relevant legislation, notarized copies of case-law supporting the pertinent legislation, an original birth certificate for Ernesto Iguarez Flores, signed by a doctor, copies of the boat's registration documents and proof of the military officer's Navy credentials." Octavian snapped open his briefcase, withdrew a thick manila folder, and flicked it onto the desk so that it slid directly into Walcott's lap.

Walcott didn't like this either, but he picked up the folder and weighed it in his palm, crossing and uncrossing his legs all the while. Then he perked up a little. "Are you aware that visa wait times in this country can stretch into the months?"

"Not if you use the powers invested in you and give us a decision right here, right now. What do you say, Mr. Walcott?"

"I'm going to need to talk to my supervisor. Could I ask you gentlemen to step into the waiting area?"

I nodded at Octavian and we rose to leave. Our conversation seemed to have caused the man genuine gastrointestinal stress. If we'd stayed any longer he probably would have crapped on the floor.

We walked back out to the lobby and gave each other significant looks that meant nothing. The receptionist was still filing her nails. People – lots of them – still mouldered in line with hot mad faces. The carpet on the floor was full of dust. Clearly the interior of the place had seen better days. We sat down in some plastic chairs by the front door.

"Do you have an appointment?" called the receptionist, a black Cuban lady with a mouth full of lipstick.

"We just saw Mr. Walcott. We have a request for a citizenship certificate," I said.

The receptionist narrowed her eyes. "I don't think we handle those. You should probably wait until you get back to Canada."

"Excuse my friend, Señora," said Octavian silkily. "Our passports seem to have been stolen. Mr. Walcott asked us to step outside for a minute. He had to consult with his supervisor. May I ask who that would be?"

"That would be Anna Velasquez," said the receptionist, indifferent again. "I'll call you when she's ready."

"What did you think? Will he go for it?" I whispered.

"Walcott has never gone for anything in his life, except maybe a colonoscopy. Whoever the boss is will make the decision. If they actually read the statutes and case law I don't think that they'll have much of a choice. The rules are clear."

"Yes, I know the rules are clear, Octavian, you patronizing prick. I'm the one who taught you about the loophole in the first place. I'm asking what the plan is if they say 'no'."

"We'll fight it out in court. We'll get administrative review."

"What about Ramón?" I said.

"What about him?"

There wasn't much else to say. I watched the people in line. My brain ached for my phone, but I'd forgotten it back at the hotel. I could almost feel the keypad under my fingers. When the ache subsided I wished I had a magazine. The chair had uneven legs. Octavian sat as straight as ever, his arms folded over his chest.

"Nervous?" I said.

"Let's not talk, Walter. I'd prefer to avoid unnecessary contact with you."

Very well then. I got up and found the bathroom, which bore the grime of decades of waiting. After five minutes I got up and went again.

"Can't you sit still?" hissed Octavian.

"So you are talking to me."

"Marycarmen. Did you tell her about *The Dancing Gorilla* playing at the Bodeguita del Medio? About my video shoots in Miami?"

"I told Mags. You know he can't keep his mouth shut."

"She thinks we'll be married within the year. She has a house in Miami all picked out. She literally called the owner and scheduled a viewing."

"So dump her."

"Dump her hell. Now she knows I'm a producer. I can't kill all of you."

"Maybe it's time you unveiled your secret profession to the world. What's the big deal, anyway?"

Octavian glared at me. He fished into his pocket, withdrew a blue object, and waved it in my face.

"Is that my passport?"

"Yes. Two can play at the game of luggage thief. Did you know that there's an international black market for passports?"

"Give it back!"

"Why? You like Cuba. If a Colombian drug lord stole your identity you would probably be detained here until the end of time. Did you know that Guantanamo Bay is literally just around the corner?"

"Give it!" I shouted.

We'd been fighting in hostile whispers. The receptionist snapped "Quiet, please!" then apparently changed her mind and pointed to an office immediately behind her. "Ms. Velasquez will see you now."

ഉഉ

Anna Velasquez's office was much larger and brighter than pink pallid Derek Walcott's, with a parquet floor and red curtains, and the Amazon warrior behind the desk inside it didn't waste any time with pleasantries.

"Have a seat, please," said Anna Velasquez. She was the physical opposite of her colleague: large and tanned with straight black hair cut in a fringe. The row of jungle-looking plants behind her on the window ledge added to the general impression of a warrior queen.

"Good afternoon, Ms. Velasquez," said Octavian, mimicking her brisk tone exactly. It was a technique he often used for getting his own way. "I gather you've had the chance to look into the matter of citizenship for our clients."

"I've looked into it alright. You must think you're very clever."

"If only my professors had agreed," said Octavian suavely, but the old snake charm had no effect whatsoever.

"We don't have the authority to grant your request. Sorry," she said, evidently not sorry at all.

"I think the law says otherwise," I said.

"Do you disagree with our interpretation of the statutes?" said Octavian.

She shrugged. "Not really. But we have a pretty narrow mandate here. Most of what we do involves visa applications. To get the green light for what you're asking we would have to talk to Citizenship and Immigration."

"Your mandate is wide enough to issue passports. I know that for a fact. Your colleague Derek Walcott told me so."

"This particular application would proceed under a special stream."

"And what stream would that be?"

"I am not under one of your cross-examinations here, sir. But I will tell you that, no, a couple of lawyers playing games probably won't be a priority around here."

"I see," I said. "So you think this is all a game. I can assure you that our clients don't think it's a game."

"I sympathize with your clients' situation, I really do. But I'm afraid it's just not our policy to do citizenship certificates on demand."

"Fine," said Octavian. "Can you give me a rough estimate of how long the file would take to process?"

"Months. Years."

"Years?" I said.

"How about we speed things up a little?" said Octavian. "Can we call Citizenship and Immigration right now?"

"I don't think so."

"What I'm hearing from you is that your office will deliberately obstruct progress on our clients' file," said Octavian, enunciating each word with great care.

Anna Velasquez sighed. It was the same bored and disenchanted sigh that Derek Walcott had exhaled in our presence only one hour earlier, although without the queasy bouquet. "Speaking frankly, Mr. Castro," she said, "I'll tell you right now that the odds of a successful application are essentially zero. It's just impossible."

Click.

"Thank you," said Octavian with satisfaction, patting his pocket, which emitted four loud beeps. "That sound you heard was a microphone. I now have audio evidence confirming that the files administered by your office are subjected to a decision-making procedure that is reckless, arbitrary and possibly corrupt." The object in his pocket beeped again. "And the audio file has now been sent to two different remote locations, in case you decide to unlawfully confiscate my property."

Velasquez did not appear shaken in the least by Octavian's theatrics. She swivelled straight-backed on her chair to face him directly. "I don't think I have to remind you as a lawyer, Mr. Castro, that non-citizens have no rights over the decision-making process. None. And recording devices are not permitted beyond the reception desk."

"Search and seize me then," said Octavian. "And may I remind you that our clients' son is not a non-citizen. Your office has a clear obligation to furnish citizens with travel documents. We're only asking you to do your job."

Any mildness had disappeared from the woman's face. "I'll have to ask you to leave now. The application fails, on the basis of insufficient information."

"I didn't come all the way to Cuba to play games," said Octavian, abandoning the conciliatory approach completely. "I don't have any problem at all pursuing this matter in the courts. It's all the same to me, I don't have to pay legal fees. You'll be ping-ponging back between Havana and Ottawa for years."

She blew out another sigh. "What's the real deal here? Are –" she glanced at the file – "Ramón and Estella. Are they your relatives?"

"I can't breach lawyer-client confidentiality, Ms. Velasquez."

"And I can't help you until you tell me the whole truth."

"The truth is that baby Ernesto Iguarez Flores is a legal citizen of Canada by federal statute."

"I think this interview is over," said Anna Velasquez.

I laid a business card on her big empty desk. "Thank you for your time, Ms. Velasquez," I said.

"If you have any questions about the case, please don't hesitate to call," said Octavian.

She smiled coldly. "Have a nice day," she said, but what she quite obviously meant was that she hoped both of us died.

♀♀

We left without saying very much. Outside there was a sweet breeze blowing westward, so good in the lungs after the sweat-ridden, tense air of the embassy. I immediately spotted Ramón sitting in his Peugeot across the street and waved. He waved back and started the car. He had probably been waiting there all day: there were twin patches of sweat under the arms of his short-sleeved shirt and he had the dark under-eye circles of a man dehydrated.

"Well," he said as we climbed into the backseat, with a small flash of his white grin, "long day, hey?"

"Unbelievably long," I said.

"Very long day," said Octavian.

"But a good day," he said cautiously, scanning both of our faces in the rear-view mirror. After holding my gaze for a moment his smile faded.

"I see," he said. "I see how it went. You don't have to tell me nothing. You bullshit lawyers."

He gunned the accelerator in the milling mixed traffic of downtown Havana. I really thought he would smash the lot of us into the nearest wall or moped or doddery old Chevrolet. Instead he aimed the car at an elderly female pedestrian, clipping the immense bag of vegetables she was carrying with his fender. She screamed something at him in Spanish. The Chevrolet shrieked its horn. Ramón drove on.

"Hey!" I shouted, as we whizzed past another traffic light. "What's the matter with you? You could have killed that woman."

"Ramón, my friend," said Octavian steadily. "Please be patient. We've presented your case to senior civil servants at the embassy. They are considering the matter and now we must wait. That is the nature of bureaucracy."

The beet-red muscles in Ramón's neck unclenched, but one could see that his blood was up. The man's moods changed faster than the traffic lights he ignored.

"The matter is not finished?"

"Absolutely not," said Octavian. "I assure you that this is normal. This is a complex matter and the paperwork will take time."

"Oh yeah? How much time?"

"I have an appointment to see the ambassador tomorrow. He's a friend of the family and a very smart man besides. He only has to make one phone call and you'll be on the next plane to Toronto."

"So please don't murder anyone, eh?" I said. "It won't help your case."

"Ramón," said Octavian. "May I give you some advice? You're a new papa and Baby Ernesto needs you – alive. Why don't you stay with your boy tomorrow and I'll call you the second I hear the news."

Ramón nodded. He reached behind to the backseat and took Octavian's hand, squeezing it hard. I don't know if it was a sign of affection or a threat.

When we pulled up in front of the high patio bar at the Cabos Melia, Mags was waiting for us up on the marble patio with two ash-blond toddlers in tow. He grinned and waved at Ramón, cradling his arms to signify a baby. Ramón gave him the thumbs up.

"I like Mr. Magellan," Ramón announced, his tone implying that he didn't particularly like anyone else. I wondered if he'd care to know about his cameo appearance in the erotic dream I'd had the night before.

"I'll be in touch," said Octavian.

Ramón nodded at him, threw a scowl in my direction and peeled away. As we made our way up the stairs Octavian and I each had a leg accosted by one of Mags' screaming albino cubs.

"Good work, kids. I told the kids to show you a bit of love," explained Mags, when the Peugeot was safely out of sight. "Tough luck today, amigos."

"How did you know?" I said.

"Because I'm a genius, Walter. I told you this would happen."

"The embassy people weren't very obliging," conceded Octavian. "Can I ask you something else, Mags? Is your wife a blow-up doll? For a woman who exists, she's been amazingly invisible on this trip."

"Maxine is feeding the baby," said Mags cheerfully. "And of course the embassy people weren't obliging. I told you this wouldn't work. I told you from the beginning. Alright kids. Play in the grass."

The sticky dwarves tore away screaming and Mags led us up to one of the little wicker tables on the patio, where two chilled beers stood waiting.

"Thanks," I said gratefully. Even the mere feel of cold aluminum on my lips was enough to start my brain buzzing with pleasure.

"Alcoholic," said Octavian, but he snapped open his own can and took a long cool drink.

"Hypocrite," I said.

"What did you tell Ramón?" asked Mags.

Octavian and I exchanged winces as we recalled Ramón's eager, expectant face peering at us from the dim windows of his car.

"I told him that the application was under review," he said.

"No, you told him you had an appointment with the ambassador. Can I ask why you would say that?" I said.

"Because Ramón is a very angry man and I wanted to leave that taxi alive."

"Fair enough," said Mags, taking a swig of beer. "What will you tell him tomorrow?"

"Nothing," said Octavian. He leaned back in his chair and turned his gaze to the ocean. "I'm leaving tomorrow on the first flight to Toronto. I suggest that you do the same."

"Is that so, Octavian," I said angrily. "When were you planning on telling me?"

"I'm telling you now," said Octavian. "How much clearer did the embassy woman have to make it? She's itching to carpet-bomb this application. Coming to Cuba was our first mistake, it's too full of beach-bum bureaucrats. We should have gone straight to Pakistan where there are no mojitos and you can literally bribe everyone."

"But you told Anna Velasquez that we would fight it out in court."

"We will," said Octavian reasonably. "But not in Cuban court. We'll have to do it in Canada. You can start Monday morning, Walter."

"Fine," I said, but inside I felt a twinge of regret. Tomorrow was lobster night at the seafood restaurant. Now I wasn't sure if I would ever get to taste it. We all sat there sipping our beers in silence. The sun was low and orange on the horizon but the heat of day lingered warm on my back.

"Well," I said, "I'm off to the bar. Let's give Cuba a big champagne kiss goodbye. Not you, Octavian. You probably have to braid your mother-in-law's hair or something."

"Room. Now," ordered Octavian. "I want that money back now, Walter. No more excuses."

"Would you calm down, Octavian? It's all there in the pants I wore to the marina."

Mags looked incredulous. "And that's it?" he said. "You're just going to leave Ramón and Estella in the dust? You're going to take their money and run? That's the kind of man you are, Octavian? Walter?"

"What do you mean 'take their money'?" said Octavian, testy under Mags' hot pop-eyed stare. "I didn't steal it. You may not know this, Mags, but it's customary for lawyers to charge a retainer against future services –"

"*We. We* didn't steal it. It's my money too," I reminded him.

"– and that retainer was fair value for my time, which, unlike yours, Mags, isn't free – or should I say worthless?" continued Octavian. "What? Why are you looking at me like that? I like Ramón. I'll tally up the billable hours and refund him whatever's left over. Do you think I wanted this to fail? I've run out of cards to play, amigo. I told Ramón that there were no guarantees. Did he listen? No. He almost killed us this afternoon. It's all shot to hell."

"Your nerves are shot to hell, Octavian," said Mags. "You give up too fast."

"I do not. But I know when to hold and when to fold."

"Do you have a better idea, Mags?" I said.

"As a matter of fact, yes," said Mags coolly, stretching out on his leather seat with his drink like a sated lion. "I have a great idea. Would you like to hear it? If so, my commission is fifty percent, thank you."

Octavian and I exchanged a glance. The sun was setting behind Mags' head. There was a chorus of screams. Somewhere in the distance one of his offspring was punching the other one to death.

"Are you serious?" said Octavian.

"Of course I'm serious. Hey! Kids! Stop fighting! Now!"

"Well played, Mags. I don't know what kind of a man I am, but we know what kind of a man *you* are. Now we're just haggling over your price," said Octavian.

"I'm not the one who went around making promises to desperate people," shot back Mags.

"Twenty percent," I said.

Mags snorted. "I need to go and play catch with my kid."

"Forty percent," said Octavian sharply. "Walter volunteers to give you half of his share. This had better be brilliant."

"Absolutely not," I said. "I do not consent."

"You owe me," said Octavian to me. "I saved your soggy diaper from Marycarmen's father the other night, and you know it. I guarantee you that your legs would have been broken."

"No one asked you for help," I said.

"And no one's asking you now. Your contribution to this enterprise has been precisely zero. Negative, if you count the fact that you forced Marycarmen's company on the rest of us. You're useless."

"Wow. I've never had two boys fight over me before," said Mags, fanning himself with a coaster like a dowager queen. He took another sip of beer. "Octavian, that was a very rude thing to say. But I accept."

"Done and done," said Octavian. They shook on it.

"You can't cut me out of my own deal!"

"You can only bargain when you actually have something to offer," said Octavian. "Spill it, Mags."

"It's nothing personal, Walter," said Mags earnestly. "It's just that I'm trying to be more assertive. This trip has really helped me grow."

I opened my mouth to say something cutting. My brain came up null. I wasn't overly perturbed by the prospect of lost income: at this point it looked like my share of any future venture was twenty percent of zero. But I was tired of both of them, of the Cabos Melia resort, of my own impotency. I missed marijuana. I even missed my mother. Mags silently pushed another beer across the table. I couldn't think of any other riposte than to drink it.

"The plan is pretty simple," he said. "We'll hit them with a lawsuit. An extremely frivolous one."

"That's it?" exploded Octavian. "That's the brilliance of your strategy? That was my idea five minutes ago."

"Wearing down a bureaucrat just takes a certain amount of willpower," said Mags patiently. "Think about it. This Anna Velasquez lady has exactly nothing riding on the outcome of this decision, but she knows one thing for sure: fulfilling your request will take a lot of work. She'll have to make phone calls. She'll have to read statutes. Why would she want to do that? Civil servants don't like work, and they absolutely hate work that they've never seen before. You have to fix it so that it's more work for her to say no than it is for her to say yes."

"But why a lawsuit? What good will it do?" I said.

"Precisely. Prolonged sun exposure has taken the edge off that fine brain of yours, Mags. You're now officially dumber than Walter," said Octavian.

"Shut up, Octavian!"

"Wait and see," said Mags. "Just trust me. Now tell me exactly what Anna Velasquez said. Word-for-word." He looked strangely blissful. There was dandruff all over his shoulders. That idiot was somehow never happier than when he was cooking up loopholes.

ΩΩ

The next morning I stumbled out of my room after a brief sleep filled with nightmares in which I wore filthy Punic-era slave rags and served Octavian, who was a pharaoh. I'd made an unpleasant discovery after dinner last night: Ramón's retainer money in its neatly pressed packet wasn't in my trouser pockets after all. It was gone.

Perhaps it fell out of my pockets during my manic-depressive taxi ride to the Marina Hemingway. Perhaps the chain-wearing, chain-smoking, gorilla-grunting driver had robbed me. In the inmost recesses of my brain, however, there was no such equivocating: I had been finely suckered by that hooker Mariela, who had snaked her skinny arms so snugly around my waist, her thumbs working like probes. I don't know if Bill was her oppressor or her accomplice, and it really didn't matter: Octavian was going to chop me into little bits, and Mags would probably eat them.

Mags spotted me and waved me over to the big window in the lobby of the Cabos Melia, where he was standing with Octavian. It was the first time in years I'd seen him wear an article of clothing that wasn't a free T-shirt. He'd borrowed one of Octavian's sleek dark suits, but he was a few inches shorter and several pounds lighter than Octavian was, so the suit bagged and sagged strangely around his shoulders and ankles like a sorcerer's robe. He looked like a wizard covered in snowflakes.

"Don't you ever wash your hair, Mags?" said Octavian crossly. "That's high-grade worsted wool you're moulting on."

Mags only grinned vaguely in response. Jibes about his appearance never perturbed him. He was preoccupied with shuffling a deck of papers that he'd somehow managed to cover with dense legal text over the course of the night. Octavian was buffing his shoes.

"And where were you after dinner last night, Walter?" said Mags. "We were up half the night working on this."

I'd been outside combing every inch of the Cabos Melia grounds for the wad of stolen cash, that's where I'd been, and when that had failed I'd been in the bathroom flushing my own head down the toilet.

"Shirking as always. You were supposed to return some stolen goods. Where's the money?" said Octavian.

"Well, Octavian, it's like this –"

"You're being suspiciously cagey about this. If you've spent even one cent over your share, you're dead," said Octavian, without looking up.

"I didn't spend the money. You think I would steal your share?"

"Come on," said Mags from behind a folder, "that was needlessly insulting. Apologize, Octavian."

"I didn't steal it. Someone stole it from me. I must have left it in that goddamn taxi at the Marina Hemingway. I was half asleep and that taxi driver must have stiffed me for it. I swear to you, that's how it was. You saw how he drove off like a maniac. I've been looking for it all morning, and it's gone. Go ahead and search all of my things if you want."

Mags slammed his folder into the wall.

"Weak. He spent it in Varadero," sneered Octavian.

"Really? Then what exactly did I buy there? Do you see a fourth-hand bicycle anywhere? A truckload of rice and beans? Hundreds of shell necklaces? Think, Octavian. There's nothing to buy in Varadero. If you don't believe me go there yourself. I swear to you I lost it."

"For pity's sake, Walter," said Mags. "Call the taxi company and see if you can get it back."

"Oh, that's a fine idea, Mr. Magellan," said Octavian bitingly. "Morals are fine in a country where everyone can afford them. This fool is lying. Even if he's telling the truth we'll never see that money again."

"Just my luck. The second I get in on a deal, there's no money in it. Well, Octavian, you get what you pay for. For Christ's sake, Walter," said Mags.

"I only have one thing to say to you, Walter. After today, you are fired. Your stake in this operation is now zero." Octavian gave his shoe a final rub and stalked out of the lobby, banging the door behind him so hard that the concierge shot him a tense look.

"Mags, it was an accident, I swear," I said. "I'll find the money. I'll make it up to you, I promise. Just tell me what we need to do. What's the plan?"

Mags wouldn't even meet my eyes. He coldly handed me a briefcase. "I don't have time to explain now. There's our taxi now. Take this briefcase and do not lose it. When I need it, I'll ask for it."

Outside it was another clear, perfect, bright-blue-skied day, of which Cuba seemed to have an endless supply. The taxi was a bright shiny Korean model – nearly all of the tourist cars were new and Asian – and when the driver discharged himself to open the doors he appraised the three of us in our big suits and briefcases and whistled. The effect was only slightly dampened by the fact that our suits and accessories were so voluminous that when we packed ourselves into the backseat we were practically cuddling.

This time we didn't bother waiting in line. Octavian slipped behind the building and paid a janitor who'd been smoking a cigarette there a C.U.C. or two to sneak us directly into the reception area through the back entrance. Not a soul in line or otherwise objected to our sudden appearance: a correctly cut power suit is like a magic passport into officialdom, and the receptionist with the mouth full of red lipstick didn't recognize us anyway. Miraculously, she was still filing her nails.

"We have an appointment to see Anna Velasquez," said Octavian in the voice of a starship commander. "I'm afraid we're five minutes late, could we just go right in?"

"I'll just let her know you're here, Mr. –" said the receptionist, reaching for the phone.

"Harper," said Octavian.

"Mr. Harper," she said, and listened to the receiver for a minute. "You can go ahead in."

Anna Velasquez met us at the door, wearing the same clothes and the same humourless expression as the day before. Now that her body wasn't hidden by a desk I could see her calf muscles bulging through flesh-toned stockings and thought with some regret of my own hairless stalks, which had the muscle tone of pudding. Her face clouded over when she saw who we were.

"Very funny," she said. "Is giving out fake names what they're teaching at law school these days?"

"I'm terribly sorry, the receptionist must have made a mistake," said Octavian, slipping past her carelessly. "But since we're here anyway, could we sit down?"

"No."

Octavian took a seat. "Thank you."

"There are more of you today," observed Anna Velasquez.

"I promise you we'll be brief, Madam Program Director," said Mags, extending a hand. "Ferdinand Magellan. I'm very pleased to meet you." Velasquez bent over and shook not only his hand but his entire frail body, and from the vaguely satisfied look on her face it was probably intentional.

"Mr. Magellan is an immigration law expert," I said. "He'll give you his card. We asked him to come in today in the event that you might care to consult him about the paperwork we submitted yesterday on behalf of our clients, Ramón Iguarez and Estella Flores."

"What you're doing is abusing the system. You need to wait your turn for your application to be processed just like anyone else," she said, sitting heavily behind the desk and staring at the back wall, clearly hoping that it would collapse on Mags.

"We waited in line just like everyone else," said Octavian. "It's not illegal to check on the status of an application."

"What my colleague means," said Mags, cutting him off, "is that I'm sure you'll allow that this is an unorthodox case. I don't need to tell you that the resolution of this matter is of paramount importance to our clients. I might be able to offer you some free insights into the legal arguments. It might speed things up a little and save you a lot of work, Madam Program Director."

"I don't need any free insights, thank you," said Velasquez irritably. "And I've read the application, by the way. I don't know who you think you are, but I know for a fact that your little boat is not equipped as a medical facility. These are people's lives you're playing with. You could have killed that woman."

"Very well," said Mags, rising to leave. "Thank you for your time," he said politely. Velasquez allowed him a slight nod.

"Not so fast," said Octavian. He clicked open his briefcase, withdrew the tome of papers that was the lawsuit and flung it like a challenge on the big oaken desk. "Ms. Velasquez, consider yourself served. We're suing you *in loco parentis* for Ernesto Iguarez Flores over anticipated breach of fiduciary duty for the comments you made yesterday about your intention to derail a completely lawful application under the *Citizenship and Immigration Act*. As you can see, we're asking for special damages as well as punitive damages. The document underneath it is an application for financial transparency under the *Freedom of Information Act*. I think I'm not the only person interested in how funds are being appropriated – or misappropriated – around here."

"Now Octavian," said Mags, wagging a finger as if in warning.

Velasquez picked up the document and read it with gritted teeth, flipping one page after the next with the tiniest possible patch of her index finger as though to minimize the risk of infection. Finally she pronounced, "This is ridiculous. This is completely frivolous."

"It is provocative," agreed Mags. "It's not necessarily the course I would have advised, Octavian. You'll only incur further delay. What I'd suggest is administrative review, if and when Ms. Velasquez renders her decision."

"There," she said. "Listen to your immigration expert. Even he's telling you that your lawsuit is ridiculous."

"What else can I do," said Octavian, his pitch escalating, "when Ms. Velasquez has categorically said that she intends to kill this application, regardless of what the law says?"

Velasquez studied him intently. "What is that you want, Mr. Castro?"

"I've told you what we want. I want a citizenship certificate for my client's son, fair and square," said Octavian.

"I'll say this exactly once before I terminate this meeting, gentlemen. What you are proposing is outrageous, unsafe and probably illegal. One of you must have the intelligence to understand that I could never allow it." She paused, looking pointedly at Mags. "I process regular immigration claims. I also have the authority to approve temporary visitor visas. That's it. If you want some guidance on those topics, I can and will give it to you. But let me tell you something else. I've been doing this job long enough to know that you're not telling me the whole story. Why are you doing this? Are these people relatives of yours?" She pronounced the words with a peculiar emphasis, still looking at Mags.

Why indeed. Money. Debt. Desperation. Unemployment. Rampant stupidity.

"Alright, Ms. Velasquez," said Mags. He was silent for a moment. "I'll level with you. We haven't told you the full story. I'm going to remember what you just said about temporary visitor visas, and then I'm going to ask you to be open-minded about what I'm about to say. On that understanding, may I proceed?"

"And I'm going to ask you to remember what you said about being brief."

"Octavian, may I?" he said.

"I suppose there's no choice," said Octavian sadly.

"A little less than a year ago, my colleague Mr. Castro visited Cuba on holiday," said Mags. "He met Ramón Iguarez and Estella Flores at the Cabos Melia resort, where he befriended them both. Some months later, a child was born on a Canadian military ship at the Marina Hemingway here in Cuba. Mr. Ramón Iguarez believes the child is his own. Do I make myself clear?"

Anna Velasquez snorted. "I suspected as much," she said. "You do realize, I hope, that if what you're saying is true the baby qualifies for citizenship automatically? That's assuming that Mr. Castro here is even a citizen."

"Mr. Castro is a citizen," said Mags smoothly. "But Ramón Iguarez has signed the birth certificate."

"Ramón is a good man," muttered Octavian. "He's always wanted to immigrate to Canada. Applying as the child's guardian might be his only chance."

She was openly leering now. "You're feeling a little guilty, I take it, Mr. Castro? I suppose I would be too, if I'd knocked up my friend's wife. Aren't you a naughty boy."

Octavian hung his head.

"And you've decided that Canadian citizenship is a consolation prize for making poor Ramón Iguarez into a cuckold," continued Velasquez. "Lawyers. What a witty bunch you are. I bet you're charging him for this too."

"Octavian, are you kidding me?" I blurted out.

"Well," said Mags, pushing his chair back. "There you have it. I have to hand it to you, Ms. Velasquez, you're a very impressive woman. You saw right through us. I guess you're not the boss around here for nothing."

The Amazon features actually softened a little. Octavian peeped up at her boyishly and managed to look a little foolish. I stood back and looked actually foolish. Nobody had told me about this turn of events. "Do you need the briefcase now?" I said.

"No, not just now," said Mags. "Thank you, Walter."

"Are you seeking custody of this child, Mr. Castro?" said Anna Velasquez.

"Not at all," said Octavian truthfully.

"Of course you aren't. You're consistent, I'll give you that."

"If word gets out about this loophole in the immigration law community, I think you can safely expect a flood of new applications. Your workload will triple," warned Mags.

"That's the first point you've made that I wholeheartedly agree with," she said. "Because I could frankly care less about Mr. Castro's extracurricular activities. But we had a budget cut last year that forced us to cut two staff, with the result that we now have an eight-week backlog of work. I don't need this right now. The system is overburdened as it is."

"So what do you propose?" said Octavian.

"I propose that you withdraw the application and withdraw the lawsuit. Then I propose that you all leave my office," she said, addressing the wall, which remained stubbornly erect.

"And in the alternative?" said Mags.

"Temporary visitor visas," said Anna Velasquez shortly. "I'm authorized to approve them."

Mags shrugged. "What else have you got?"

"Don't push it, Mr. Magellan."

"Do you have contacts in Citizenship and Immigration who have authority over the marriage sponsorship program?"

"Why?" she said, smirking horribly at Octavian. "Don't tell me you want to marry her now."

Octavian passed an arm over his face. "I just don't know any more. I'm confused."

"If such an application were to be put forth," said Mags, "could you give me your contact's name and a letter vouching for my safe passage through the system?"

"Only if those are the absolute last words out of your mouth."

Mags made a gesture of zipping his lips shut. "Temporary visitor visas. We'll take three," he said. "For the husband, the wife and the child."

"I have no idea what Mr. Castro could possibly hope to achieve with all three of them," said Velasquez. "And I don't care."

"Two years each," said Mags.

"Ridiculous. I can't do a two-year tourist visa."

"Then no deal."

"One year. Even that will raise a lot of eyebrows. If you even try a refugee claim, I'll have all of them deported. That's the best I can do for you. I mean that, Mr. Magellan."

Mags looked at Octavian. Octavian looked at me. I looked at both of them and nodded with simulated wisdom.

"We'll take it," said Mags.

"And you'll abandon any claims for citizenship-by-boat," said Anna Velasquez. "Not to mention your ridiculous lawsuit."

"Agreed," said Octavian.

"Fine," said Anna Velasquez, exhaling with evident relief. "Done. We'll get the papers drawn up right away. One of the consular assistants will take care of it for you. Now promise me one more thing."

"What?" said Mags.

She looked at him as though he was a worm that had slimed its way out of her lunch apple, and slowly shook her head. "The people of Cuba have enough problems without lawyers breeding on the island. Please don't ever come back to this embassy."

QQ

I was still confused when we left the embassy two hours later. The three of us had waited in the dark humid air of the corridor by the reception desk, saying little as we strained our bottoms on the hard metal chairs and watched the queue of people limp slowly forward like a millipede on crutches. Roughly once an hour an argument in agitated Spanish would erupt between a line-weary Cuban and one of the embassy officials, but otherwise the hall was stiffly silent.

"Octavian," I said, "did you really knock up —"

Octavian and Mags burned me in unison with looks that could melt steel, so I clapped my mouth shut.

At long last the receptionist beckoned us over. Wordlessly she handed Mags a bound folder and then dropped her attention back to the infinitely absorbing task of chiselling her fingertips.

Mags shuffled through the contents of the folder, gave a little satisfied smile, and said, "It's all here. I think we're free to leave, gentlemen."

We walked down Calle 30 under the cool relief of the palm trees that stretched as high as the three-storey apartment blocks lining the street. Every few blocks someone would lean a dark head over a balcony and hoot at us in Spanish, probably to inform us how stupid we were to sport wool suits in Havana. Only when the embassy was safely out of sight did we make eye contact and nod, as if giving each other permission to speak.

"Taxi, or a walk first?" said Mags. He breathed deeply and held his right leg in a poorly executed yoga pose. "I have a leg cramp from sitting on that torture chair. Maybe I'll get a massage tonight."

"Let's walk," said Octavian. "There's no big rush to get back to the resort. We can have a drink in Parque Lennon. I'll take a picture of you sitting with Lennon so you can show it to your kids."

"How about a snack? That embassy was like an oven inside. I'm parched," said Mags, stopping in front of a tropical array of ice creams in a shop window.

Octavian shook his head and nudged him forward. "No ice cream with your constitution, Ferdinand. Keep marching and stick to bottled water. You don't have my invincible third-world stomach."

"You could have at least warned me," I burst out. "Couldn't you have told me what was going on? I looked like a jerk in there."

"Sorry about that, Walter," said Mags. He gazed back longingly at the ice cream shop, but Octavian walked briskly ahead. "I would have told you everything. But it's your own fault. You disappeared last night when we were working out the lawsuit."

"I was trying to find the money. And you didn't even file the lawsuit!"

"People are terrified of lawsuits. If you want to get someone's attention, just sneak up behind them and say 'lawsuit'. Without the lawsuit she wouldn't have given us the time of day."

"What about the kid?"

Mags shrugged. "What about him?"

"Octavian. That kid isn't really yours, is it?"

Octavian laughed at me through his movie-star mirrored shades.

"Is Ernesto your kid or not?"

"That answer is lawyer-client privileged, Walter," said Mags, winking strenuously up at the tips of the palm trees. "And frankly, it's better for my professional ethics and yours if I don't ever learn the answer. Did you enjoy my game of 'bait the bureaucrat', by the way?"

"I thought we were playing good lawyer-bad lawyer," said Octavian. "And who said Ernesto was my kid?"

"I certainly didn't," said Mags. "I didn't say anything of the sort."

"Could somebody please explain to me what just happened in there?" I said. "What about the loophole?"

"The universe is an infinity of loopholes," said Mags philosophically. "As it turns out, we'll be using a different one than originally planned. When Estella and Ramón arrive in Canada on their freshly minted tourist visas they can file for permanent residency. After that it's a hop, skip and a jump to citizenship."

"You can't just do that, Mags," I said. "I remember that much from the Benitez file. You can't just enter the country as a tourist and then skip to citizenship. It's impossible."

Mags turned around to look at Octavian, who'd been trailing us a little to admire an ebony-skinned fortune-teller in the street. She was wearing an elaborate ruffled dress and shuffled a deck of cards in a manner that was strangely alluring. "Doesn't he know?" said Mags.

"We were busy all night. When would I have had time to tell him?" said Octavian, without looking away from the fortune-teller. "He was busy, too. Pissing away our money."

"I swear to you that cabbie robbed me!"

"I see," said Mags to me. He stopped and looked at me earnestly. "Listen, Walter. To expedite the process Estella and Ramón will have to divorce and marry Canadian citizens. Luckily, divorce is fast and easy in Cuba and now that we have those tourist visas the whole thing is as easy as pie. It's one thing to try and bring over a spouse without any papers, but when someone is legally in the country already – even as a tourist – it really changes the game. It's like a vote of confidence from the civil service. Bureaucrats love that stuff."

"Oh, is that all, Mags?" I snarled. "A simple case of marriage fraud. And how do you plan to find Canadian citizens willing to commit marriage fraud for a couple of Cubans, one whom is about a hair away from killing us all?"

"We've already found them," said Mags. He gave Octavian a quick sidelong glance.

"Oh yeah? Who?"

"You," said Octavian, smiling horribly. "Us, actually. It's the perfect solution. Ramón wants to get his family out of Cuba. I want to get out of the engagement mess you created with Marycarmen. If I marry Estella we'll be killing two birds with one stone."

"And what about me?"

"You lost our retainer – you claim – but at least this way we'll get the rest of the paycheque. By 'we' I mean me and Mags, of course. You've already cost us more than your share. By marrying Ramón you'll just about make up for it."

I stopped walking and turned to face him open-mouthed.

"Be reasonable, Walter. Someone has to marry Ramón, or how is he supposed to get his immigration papers?" said Mags sensibly. "Same-sex unions are perfectly legal in Canada. If anything, a same-sex marriage should make the claim more interesting. If they try and block the application, we'll make a big stink in the newspapers on the grounds of homophobia. The powers that be don't want to lose the left-wing vote. Now that would be a good time."

"It most certainly would not be a good time!" I hissed at him. A group of bare-chested men playing dominoes in the shade of an ancient pickup truck stopped their game to stare at us. "Are you out of your mind? I'm not having a fake visa marriage to a man!"

"Walter, can you keep your voice down please?" said Octavian. "Estella is a very attractive lady. After I tell Marycarmen – who *you* dragged to Cuba, may I remind you – about my wife Estella and our illegitimate child, even she won't be able to ignore it. She'll break our engagement and with any luck she'll be out of my life forever. Her family will congratulate themselves on their narrow escape from a marriage of shame and sacrifice a bull to the Pope or something. It's perfect, actually. We all go home happy."

"Everyone except me! I refuse to do it! I will not go through with this!'

"Fine," said Mags. "Then give Ramón his money back. All of it."

"I can't," I said, my teeth starting to chatter. I was really panicking now. "I lost it. You know I lost it. That taxi driver stole it. Mags, please."

"Then prepare to be disbarred. If Ramón tells the embassy that you gave him a cock-and-bull story about the *Canadian Naval War Act*, took his money and skipped town, Anna Velasquez will call the Law Society and your career as a lawyer will be over. In fact, not only would she make the call, I have a feeling that she'd really enjoy it. You can't back out of this deal now, Walter, you have to find a way to make it work. You've violated almost every single rule of professional conduct in the book during this trip. I warned you, Walter. You didn't listen to me. No one ever does."

If my arms hadn't been sore under the weight of the stupid briefcase, I would have throttled him. "And you don't think staging a fake homosexual marriage to your own client is against the rules of professional conduct? What if Ramón doesn't want to go through with it?"

"Of course it is," shrugged Mags, flapping the wings of his baggy suit like a broken bird. "But after breaking so many rules, what's one more? Anyway, *I'm* certainly not intending to fake-homosexually marry anyone. I didn't even advise it in my professional capacity. I'm only making general remarks about the process of gaining citizenship. If you choose to take them out of context, that's your problem. As for Ramón, he'll do anything to get out of Cuba. God knows what they have on him here. He'll go through with it."

I was pouring with sweat. "Help me, Mags. This whole thing was your idea, you must have another loophole up your sleeve. What about your ethics? You lied to Anna Velasquez. You told her that Ernesto was Octavian's kid."

"I absolutely did not," said Mags indignantly. "I hereby solemnly swear and affirm that every word that came out of my mouth in that embassy was absolutely and verifiably correct. I also affirm that Anna Velasquez was free to conclude anything she wished from what I said. I wasn't there at the moment of conception, were you? Have you seen a DNA test? Has Octavian ever denied it in your hearing?"

"Mags speaks the truth," said Octavian. "I have never denied being the father of Ernesto Iguarez Flores."

Lawyers are occasionally required to engage in gymnastic feats of doublethink in order to keep their sense of ethics pristine, and while Octavian merely dabbled in the sport from time to time, Mags was the master of it. He had genuinely convinced himself that, because there was no definite proof to the contrary, Baby Ernesto might very well be Baby Octavian. If life was a video game, Mags had just become a Level 1000 lawyer with warlock powers of deception and I was powerless against him and his flawless inane logic.

Octavian laid a hand on my shoulder. "And just so you know, Walter, you are legally required to consummate the gay marriage," he said. "That's right there in the *Canadian Naval War Act* too. Tell him, Mags."

"He is not," said Mags kindly. "Any marriage that may or may not take place would occur entirely on paper, Walter – not that I'm advocating such a thing, I'm just acknowledging its theoretical possibility. It's not a bad thing. And who knows? You might like it. Sometimes marriage comes first and love comes later. But if not, the marriage might not even have to last that long, if Anna Velasquez's connections are as good as she says they are."

"I veto this plan," I said firmly. "I say we stick with the original loophole."

"The original loophole is dead," said Mags. "It was always dead. You can't say I didn't warn you. It was a very dumb loophole."

"And kindly remember something else, Walter," said Octavian. "In case you're thinking of skipping town and abandoning your partners, not to mention your clients, I have your passport."

"You would maroon me in Havana."

"You robbed me," Octavian reminded me. "And you lost and/or stole our entire retainer. If you want to be the one to tell Ramón that he'll have to stay in Cuba alone without his wife and child, be my guest."

We had reached Parque Lennon now, and there he was: John Lennon, bespectacled and long-haired in the trees, sitting in bronze on a bench like he'd been expecting me for a long time. I sat down in the crook of his arm and thought wistfully about Basu, who had died so thoughtlessly. Basu was at fault, and my mother doubly so, with her blind urging for a successful lawyer son – and so was Marycarmen with her sinister beauty, and Mariela with her funereal hooker eyes, and Mags, who had invented the accursed loophole in the first place. I regretted them all, but I regretted nothing quite as much or quite as bitterly as the day I'd met Octavian Castro.

Mags did a skinny cartwheel on the grass.

"You're embarrassing yourself, Mags," called Octavian.

"It's just a little fun," said Mags, running up to us breathless. "You've got to let loose a little. That's what a vacation is all about. Come on Walter, I'm honestly sorry for you, but you checkmated yourself. Weren't you going to get us something to drink, Octavian? I'm dying of thirst here."

"Walter, could you pass me that briefcase now?" said Octavian. I shoved it at him hard, but he only appraised me with one of his mild looks. "Come on, cheer up. It's not so bad. Marrying Ramón for a little while is a lot better than the alternative. Think of this whole thing as an adventure." He clicked open the briefcase, and I now knew why the damn thing had been so heavy. It was full to the brim with bottles of water and beer. I was no good at lawyering, but apparently I had a real talent for carrying things. More to the point: Reader, I married him.

Postmanhood: An Epilogue

Gay-marrying Ramón for immigration purposes was the definite low point of my career as a lawyer, which incidentally is now over.

When we returned to the Cabos Melia I marched directly to the much-vaunted seafood restaurant and ordered two lobster specials, a whole red snapper and eight glasses of wine. After morosely downing the lot I staggered to the beach and burped lobster clouds alone into the darkness for the next several hours. My outlook was bleak. If I were to proffer Ramón a tourist visa instead of the citizenship he'd bought so dearly, he would beat my organs out and sell them at cost. If I told Mags and Octavian to go to hell and quietly hightailed it back to Toronto, I would lose the only job I had – a moot point anyway, because Octavian clung fast to my passport. And Mags was right: Ramón was not the type of man to allow even the slightest of slights to pass un-avenged. He had my stamp and signature on half a dozen pieces of paper and it would only be a matter of time before the Law Society cleaned and gutted me. I emitted a final fishy belch and stared out into the dark water. Marriage it was, then. I would propose to Ramón.

We called Ramón the next day. I'd hoped to give him the good news about his impending nuptials at a nice safe telephone distance, but as soon as I mouthed the words "good news" and "embassy" he hung up. The man had nerves like brittle glass. Three hours later there was a message for us at the concierge's desk, instructing us to meet him that night at the Bar Cabaña in Varadero.

"A shame," said Mags ruefully. "I wanted to tell him myself. I think he trusts me. He knows I just want to help." We were lounging by the swimming pool with a couple of beers while Octavian frolicked in a tiny bathing suit at the shallow end with Mags' youngest two children, who adored him like a magus. At least two females swimming in his vicinity were visibly melting with love. There's something about a lone man with children that seems to set the feminine heart on fire.

"You really have to leave?"

"My week is up, amigo," he said. "My legal aid clients are probably all in jail by now without me to babysit them, but what the hell. What a great week it's been. I feel like a new man."

"Where's Maxine?"

Mags looked away.

"Having a post-coital nap, is that it?"

"No, Walter. Nothing like that."

"How come she never wants to meet us?"

"She's dead, Walter."

"*What?*"

It turned out that Maxine really had been imaginary: she'd actually died the year before of breast cancer, and as Mags had retreated into daycares and nannies and an elaborate web of deceit, too despondent to tell anyone the truth, the lie had slipped out of his control. He shyly asked if I was angry at him.

"Not at all," I said awkwardly. "I'm so sorry, Mags." But neither of us knew what else to say after that, so we shook hands and he went back to the hotel to board the shuttle bus to the airport. In a hundred years I never would have guessed that I would never see Mags again.

When Octavian and I got to the bar that night, Ramón was smoking outside on the street. The moon shone like silver into Ramón's eyes, which were moist and pooled with blood at their corners.

"Good or bad," he said, with a gleam of a white grin. "That's all I want to know, Octavian, *asere*."

"Good, I think," I said uncertainly.

"Good. As good as you can get under the circumstances," said Octavian.

"I don't like it," announced Ramón. "I like things to be black or white. Is my son a Canadian or not? He cannot be half a Canadian. He is or he is not."

"He could be. It depends on you. Let's have a drink together, my treat," said Octavian carefully. He caught Ramón by the arm and led him into the crowded bar, a strategy of which I wholeheartedly approved: if Ramón planned on violence, I wanted plenty of witnesses.

To his distinct discredit, Ramón seemed quite cheerful when we informed him that he'd need to temporarily divorce the mother of his child. He seemed to think he'd won a provisional get-out-of-marriage-free pass with optional sex parties. When I told him about part two of the scheme, the bit that involved a twin set of new marriages, he burst into flames.

"That is disgusting," breathed Ramón, pouring his warm half-drunken breath all over my face.

"Don't be a homophobe," said Octavian patiently. "Join the twenty-first century."

"Your whole society is sick."

"Ramón, you've been killing yourself to enter this very same sick society. In our society, marriage between two men is perfectly legal. If you don't like this idea, walk away right now. We told you we'd do our best to get you Canadian citizenship and that's exactly what we're doing."

"You are forcing me to commit the ultimate sin. You and your boat, it was all lies and bullshit. Now to save my family I must offer you my bum. This is against nature. It's against God."

"It's perfectly moral," said Octavian, jerking his head toward me. "He won't lay a finger on you until after you're married."

"You want me to become your fairy-boy," Ramón hissed at me. "That's what you were after the whole time. My ass."

"Do you honestly not comprehend the concept of a sham marriage? This is for citizenship, not sex."

"And my wife. My wife will have to marry a woman too? Disgusting. That is how citizenship works in your country, by forcing people to become perverts."

I explained that Estella would briefly contract marriage to Octavian.

"What have you done to my life?" roared Ramón. "And what am I supposed do? After this bastard marries my wife?"

"You can have her back when I'm done," said Octavian with dangerous nonchalance. "Alternatively, we'll go home and you can forget about the whole thing."

Ramón took my palm under the table and very quietly crushed it until the bone cracked. Then he kissed me long and wet on the lips, with an intensity bordering on violence.

Let it be known that the marriage was not consummated.

♋♋

If this story had been set in Hollywood rather than in the tawdry theatre of my life, the ending would have been quite predictable. Having sunk so low, the hero – or anti-hero, in this case – must seek a path to redemption. Any minute now he'll have a grand epiphany. He'll see the error of his wicked ways and practice *pro bono* for the rest of his life, using his powers of legality to rescue widows and orphans from the clutches of debt collectors and grasping landlords. He's poor but happy.

Or he'll exit the vile profession entirely. Perhaps he'll become a swimming instructor. Cue a wide-angle roaming shot of a swimming pool with children splashing happily in the pretty blue water. Walter-with-a-whistle coaches them at the butterfly stroke like a cross between their favourite mad uncle and the Rear Admiral of Marineland. He's a reformed man now; he might be poor, but on the other hand he is also destitute.

Another ending might be a classic *deus ex machina*: a Surprise Death. Mariela's pimp might jump out of the shadows and knife me, or Ramón might suddenly kick the bucket, thus rendering our journey into the loophole universe a mere postmodern piece of phantasy. All of the best authors do it: Fitzgerald with his Gatsby, Tolstoy with Anna Karenina, Turgenev with his Bazarov…and you can see that after the whole business collapsed I pinched Octavian's collection of Russian novels from his office and started reading them for lack of any better company. Authors are fond of killing off their protagonists; it is a nice clean ending to the process, and quite frankly things were so bad after I got back to Toronto that I wouldn't have minded.

Well, what of it?

After we returned to Toronto my life disintegrated. There was a brief moment of satisfaction when we volunteered to fly back with Estella and Baby Ernesto to escort them through Customs and Immigration. Ramón, who'd lingered in Havana to pack up their belongings, sentimentally took it as a gesture of conciliation. In fact Octavian had enticed Marycarmen to meet us at the airport with hints of an elaborate public marriage proposal, and then made a point of tenderly holding Estella's hand as he cantered down the Arrivals platform at Pearson airport. After volleying screams back and forth a few times in Spanish, Marycarmen's parents dragged her away weeping, and she was never to be seen again at the smell-ridden office over the Zaika restaurant. Estella seemed oddly pleased by this scene. She rather liked Octavian. She was more than a little sorry when she had to divorce him, I think.

And then Octavian vanished into thin air, leaving me alone to shovel up the mess. Ramón joined his family in Toronto and it all went just as Mags had predicted: within a year all three of them, Ramón, Estella and Baby Ernesto, were permanent residents of Canada. What Mags had failed to predict, with his usual acute grasp of the psychology of normal humans, was that Ramón's gay marriage would make him the laughingstock of the macho Toronto Cuban community.

A fraudulent marriage is a tricky matter. Octavian and Estella shared a language, a heritage and – according to the papers furnished by Anna Velasquez, anyway – even a child. Their union was so swiftly and so eagerly blessed by the Canadian Border Services Agency that the only thing missing was the Citizenship and Immigration Minister throwing rice at their honeymoon. My love affair with Ramón, however, was greeted with markedly less enthusiasm, and we had to work diligently to maintain the façade. There was no question of us living at a distance, and for one year Ramón suffered through regular excruciating visits from visa officers, who minutely probed him for details of the style of underwear I favoured, the flavour of the cake served at our wedding and the frequency and vivacity of our sex life. To make ends meet he worked night shifts under the counter at a convenience store, an arrangement which just enabled us to sleep under the same roof without Ramón effecting my murder. I spent most of our married life in hiding.

On the day his citizenship papers came through, Ramón filed for divorce. Two weeks later he called me up and demanded alimony.

"I'm not paying you alimony, Ramón. This marriage was a sham, remember?"

"Maybe," said Ramón indifferently. He now worked as a security guard for the Bank of Montréal and had only the faintest trace of a Spanish accent. "But I do not care. You humiliated me with this marriage. And now you must pay."

"I don't have any money to give you, Ramón. How can you not know that? Didn't our life together mean anything to you?"

Click.

Ramón officially reported me to the Law Society, spilling every sordid detail. I was called in to chambers for a hearing, thoroughly tongue-lashed, and shortly afterward I was suspended from the profession for three years. The tale of birth, money and wife-swapping on the high seas was so fantastic that someone at the disciplinary hearing leaked it to the press, and for a moment I was famous – or rather notorious – once again. Octavian went unscathed, on the grounds that nobody could find him.

I learned later that he hadn't gone very far. Some weeks after we arrived back in Canada, *The Dancing Gorilla* – the terrible song we'd heard playing at La Bodeguita del Medio – suddenly went platinum in Miami. Octavian had finally hit the big time. He used his profits from the song to purchase his own studio, a new house and a flash car; these emblems of success emboldened him at last to disclose his true calling to his family. Money and fame are great equalizers, and ultimately his parents and their sinister siblings were quite chuffed with the cars he bought them.

As a minor Latin music mogul, Octavian couldn't very well handle his own legal affairs anymore, so he hired the best lawyer he knew, the best lawyer any of us knew, Mr. Ferdinand Magellan. Mags quit Legal Aid and the juice-bottling factory precisely four minutes after Octavian phoned him with the offer. The rock-and-roll lifestyle of an entertainment lawyer really agreed with him. He sent me a picture of himself laughing with his children, his teeth gleaming white after an expensive set of caps had been installed to mask the damage he'd inflicted on them after years of bulimia. He looked toned, healthy-haired and happy, and some months later he related the facts as I've explained them. Last time we spoke, he was thinking of marrying again.

After Octavian left for Miami my outlook was dismal; I had a mishmash B.A. in business studies and a law degree that the Law Society had forbidden me to use under any circumstances, *ad infinitum*; moreover, I was destitute, despised and divorced.

After a couple of months festering back in my old bedroom, I approached my mother and sheepishly asked her if she might be able to call Rosa, her colleague at the post office. Rosa obliged, and I've been a postman ever since. I have a little red and white van with big open doors on both sides, and they give us very nice blue fur-lined coats to wear during the winter. There are several extremely cute cats on my route that never fail to offer up their little furry bellies for scratching, the exercise is excellent, and in a few years I'll probably have my student loan debt – which I apparently amassed for absolutely no reason at all – completely paid off. I'll never bathe in a mahogany bathtub, there is no Maserati XL 500 in my future and my wife will probably be a pock-marked leper, but I have an apartment of my own – bare and empty now that Ramón is gone – and I eat dinner with my mother three times a week. I've been on a few dates with women from around the office. In my spare time I like to stalk Bianca – we chat twice a week these days – and look up my old classmates on the Internet so that I can begrudge them their success.

A few weeks ago, Senior Mail Carrier Pat Mencken wrenched his ankle when he slipped on a loose tile he was fixing in his basement; six hours later head office asked if I would cover his route in Forest Hill, one of the city's truly posh postal codes. Splendid, I thought, we can sue the staircase manufacturer for spillions, but then I remembered that I had been disbarred from the practice of law. Still, I thought, resigning to the torpor of the here and now, in the life of a mail carrier this was a speck of enormous luck. Pat protected his territory with the ferocity of a mama bear and after two days walking it I understood him perfectly. If you overlook the haughty snap-jawed dogs, rich neighbourhoods are a mail carrier's dream: green-trimmed lawns with nary a broken stoop or staircase, fragrant sprays of lilac bush in the springtime and sweet Filipina maids and nannies peeping out to accept the latest fat statements from the bank. Now and then the lord of the manor himself will actually deign to collect his own packages and it was on one such occasion that I got the fright of my life: Blake, the varsity hockey jockey and my erstwhile law school chum, opened the door. He wasn't dressed in anything special, but he had a superb Lexus parked in the driveway and the house was the size of a galaxy. "Morning," he said pleasantly, and looking me flush in the eye he took his mail and shut the door without a hint of recognition.

Blake and I had once been as tight as drums. We'd downed vats of beer together at H. Rat's Best Pub and Pizzeria, ruminating endlessly on hockey. Later on he'd despised me, delighting in veiled comments about the wickedness of outsourcing – ironic, considering the scandal that erupted when it became known that Blake's own law firm, Sullivan Phelps, had fired several of its junior lawyers and farmed their work out to India. Now I was so insignificant I was unworthy even of his disdain; I was merely another spare part that kept the smooth apparatus of his charmed life running. I cried a little that night.

The next morning I rose at seven, to deliver Blake's mail.

Other Recent Quattro Fiction